A walk in the garden . . .

Recalling that Stephen Rutledge had only just returned from the horrors of Waterloo, Lorna reached out and laid her hand upon his sleeve.

He looked at her hand, then, without a word, he captured her fingers in his strong grasp, held them for a moment, then slowly raised them to his lips.

The major's lips were firm and warm, and the touch of them against Lorna's skin did strange things to her senses, making her wonder how those lips would feel against her own. The moment seemed to go on forever, as if suspended in time, and all was quiet save for the soft, melodious song of a bird perched on a rose trellis near the bottom of the garden.

"You cannot do it," he said, the words so soft Lorna almost did not hear them.

She had no idea what he meant by those whispered words, and still a bit bemused by the image of the major's mouth capturing hers, she was obliged to call herself back to the moment. "What can I not do?"

"You cannot marry Paul Clement."

COMING IN APRIL

The Gold Scent Bottle by Dorothy Mack

Max Waring left London after losing his fiancee—to his
father. Returning four years later, he meets the lovely
Abigail Monroe. Max has something of Miss Monroe's, and
to get her property back, Abigail must pose as Max's bride-
to-be. But pretending to be in love soon becomes more
than just a game....

0-451-20003-9/$4.99

Falling for Chloe by Diane Farr

Sylvester "Gil" Gilliland is a friend—nothing more—to his
childhood chum, Chloe. But Gil's mother sees more to
their bond. And in a case of mother knows best, what
seems a tender trap may free two stubborn hearts.

0-451-20004-7/$4.99

Breach of Promise by Elisabeth Fairchild

The village of Chipping Campden is abuzz with gossip
when the local honey merchant, Miss Susan Fairford, leases
her old home to a mysterious gentleman who calls himself
Philip Stone. Time will tell whether bachelor and beekeeper can overcome their fears in order to discover just how
much they have in common.

0-451-20005-5/$4.99

To order call: 1-800-788-6262

Miss Maitland's Letters

Martha Kirkland

A SIGNET BOOK

SIGNET
Published by New American Library, a division of
Penguin Putnam Inc., 375 Hudson Street,
New York, New York 10014, U.S.A.
Penguin Books Ltd, 27 Wrights Lane,
London W8 5TZ, England
Penguin Books Australia Ltd, Ringwood,
Victoria, Australia
Penguin Books Canada Ltd, 10 Alcorn Avenue,
Toronto, Ontario, Canada M4V 3B2
Penguin Books (N.Z.) Ltd, 182–190 Wairau Road,
Auckland 10, New Zealand

Penguin Books Ltd, Registered Offices:
Harmondsworth, Middlesex, England

First published by Signet, an imprint of New American Library,
a division of Penguin Putnam Inc.

First Printing, March 2000
10 9 8 7 6 5 4 3 2 1

 REGISTERED TRADEMARK—MARCA REGISTRADA

Printed in the United States of America

PUBLISHER'S NOTE
This is a work of fiction. Names, characters, places, and incidents either are
the product of the author's imagination or are used fictitiously, and any
resemblance to actual persons, living or dead, business establishments,
events, or locales is entirely coincidental.

*To my critique partner, Carol Otten,
who is also C. J. Card. And to the
members of the Georgia Romance Writers,
who work so hard to help make writing
a more joyous experience for all of us.*

Prologue

June 15, 1815, near Brussels, Belgium . . .

"**B**last it, Stephen," the lieutenant said, tossing his cards onto the overturned chest that served as a table, "you win again. I vow I do not know why I continue to pit my skills against yours, for you have the devil's own luck. How much do I owe you now? Is it two million or three?"

Major Stephen Rutledge shrugged his shoulders. "I lost count some time last month. Perhaps we should begin a new tally."

Lieutenant Clement made no reply, and Stephen watched as the fellow stood and stretched his slender physique, causing the unsteady camp chair to tip over and fall to the ground.

Clement paid no heed to the fallen furniture, merely stepped around it, walked the few paces to the open tent flap, and stared into the gathering dusk of the balmy June evening. Though a handsome man by anyone's standards, the gentleman's blond good looks were marred at the moment by a rather haughty expression. "I should have done better," he said, as if thinking aloud, "to have accepted the duchess's invitation for this evening's squeeze."

"What?" Stephen said in mock dismay, "and missed all this excitement?"

Paul Clement turned slightly and glanced at the

other two occupants of the tent, not bothering to hide
his disdain. Their fellow officers, both of whom had
given up on the never-ending rubbers of whist, were
now stretched out on their respective cots, and the
dull rumble of their snores echoed loud enough to
be heard halfway to the Duchess of Richmond's ball.
"Barbarians," he said.

"A harsh assessment, indeed, when they both
speak so highly of you."

The lieutenant muttered something beneath his
breath. "As usual, Stephen, you choose to make a
joke of everything, but I am persuaded that if Napoleon's troops ever do get here—an event I begin to
doubt more with each passing day—they will have
no need of rifles and ammunition."

Stephen laughed. "In other words, you expect Boney's men to find us all dead of boredom."

"Can you doubt it?"

Vouchsafing no reply, Stephen gathered up the
cards, and for want of anything better to do, he
began to shuffle them, the action fluid, the sound a
mere whisper. His hands, though large, were quick,
his fingers nimble, not unlike those of his father, who
had lived by his wits and his dubious skill at the
gaming tables.

Unfortunately, George Rutledge had run out of
luck nearly ten years before, when Stephen was in
his first year at Oxford, obliging his son to quit the
university and choose the military life.

Not that it had been a bad choice. As with everything he undertook, Stephen had made the best of
his years in the army and had gained a degree of
respect from his fellow officers, but he still had not
forgiven his father for squandering the family funds.
Not wishing to think of his parent, the man whose
dark, rugged visage had been so much like his own,
Stephen returned his attention to Paul Clement.

The lieutenant had been out of sorts since early this afternoon, just after the post arrived, and it did not require any particular mental ability to determine that he had received disquieting news. Still, when men lived in close quarters, they learned to allow one another their privacy; especially a man as prideful as Lieutenant Clement.

Determined to mind his own business, Stephen returned to the subject of the Duchess of Richmond's ball. "We have attended at least a dozen balls since we arrived in Belgium, and at none of these have you danced with even one of the young ladies presented to you. Since you insist upon being allowed to prop up the wall, a casual observer might assume you did not care for such entertainment."

"Nor do I," Paul Clement said.

"Then what makes you think this evening's affair would have proved more to your liking? Especially after last Tuesday's musicale."

When the lieutenant groaned and begged not to be reminded of that tedious evening, Stephen laughed, recalling the colonel's niece, who had been so obliging as to favor the guests with more than an hour's worth of harp solos. "After the musicale, you gave it as your opinion that there was not a fresh face or a fresh topic of conversation in the whole of Belgium. Has something occurred to soften your censure of those of our countrymen gathered in this charming country?"

For a moment, Stephen thought the lieutenant meant not to reply. He was mistaken, however, for Clement returned to the camp chair he had vacated moments before, and after righting it and seating himself, he removed a sheet of crumpled vellum from inside his tunic. "I received a letter today," he said, tossing the paper onto the makeshift table. "From my father."

Since the single sheet had been mutilated almost

beyond recognition, Stephen had no difficulty in judging it to be an unwelcome missive. "Sir Duncan is in good health, I trust."

"Never better," Clement replied, his tone dry. "Father is quite ecstatic, actually, and no wonder, for he informs me he has finally found me a wife."

"What!"

The baronet's son used the flat of his hand to iron out the crumpled letter. "It would appear that my father has pledged my troth."

Though he knew Paul Clement was not given to jests, Stephen looked to see if he was in earnest.

As if privy to Stephen's thoughts, Clement said, "Believe me, I am as good as engaged. Or should I say, 'as *bad* as engaged'?"

He raised the letter to the fading light, as if searching for a particular passage. "Here, let me share with you my father's description of my future bride." After clearing his throat, he read aloud, "Miss Maitland is a healthy female, and though not in the first blush of youth, she is well formed and not unattractive."

Not unattractive! Stephen kept to himself his suspicions about the meaning of such a dubious compliment, even when the lieutenant voiced his own misgivings.

"I suspect that such precise phrasing was meant to conceal from me the fact that my intended resembles the south end of a north-facing horse."

Undeceived by the poor attempt at humor, Stephen said, "Why would you even consider marrying a stranger? Especially if you have doubts about the young woman's desirability."

The lieutenant merely shrugged. "I should think there are always doubts. Should you be entertaining any fears for my future felicity, however, allow me to assure you—as my father assured me—that I shall like the woman prodigiously . . . that is, once I get past what he calls her natural reserve."

Stephen whistled softly. So, the female had neither beauty nor conversation.

The affianced gentleman remained silent for a few moments, perusing the letter as though he hoped it might reveal something he had previously missed. From the harsh, rigid set of his handsome jaw, his hopes were not realized, and he slowly folded the missive and returned it to his tunic. "As for Miss Maitland's many admirable qualities," he said, "my father listed them all. I shall not, however, bore you with the lot."

"Surely you will not agree to this engagement by proxy? Sir Duncan cannot expect you to—"

"I have a duty to my family, and my father expects me to fulfill it. A man like you, one who has lived by his own devices for at least a dozen years, cannot possibly understand the demands of family."

Choosing to ignore the other man's unfounded and totally erroneous assumption, Stephen said, "But what of your duty to yourself? Contentment in marriage is difficult enough to achieve even when one is allowed to follow one's heart. In a case such as this, there can be little hope of happiness."

"You cannot have been listening, my friend, for did I not tell you scarce two minutes past that my father was ecstatic?"

"It is not Sir Duncan's happiness that concerns me. His feelings upon the matter are immaterial."

Paul Clement shook his head. "You quite mistake the matter, for his sentiments are quite material." Smiling at his own pun, he added, "You will understand my parent's joy when I tell you that Miss Lorna Maitland is the only child of a wealthy wool merchant."

The lieutenant's upper lip curled ever so slightly

in distaste at the utterance of the word "merchant," leaving no doubts as to his feelings regarding his future father-in-law's connection with trade.

"As luck would have it," the future groom continued, "this particular merchant is so wishful of establishing his daughter in society that he is prepared to settle the mountain of debts accumulated by the Clement family—past and present. And all we need do to earn this quite impressive sum is to accept the female as the next Lady Clement."

Well aware of the lieutenant's sometimes overbearing pride, Stephen said, "Can you do that? Can you accept a Cit's daughter?"

"I will do what I must."

"And suppose you should fall in love with someone else?"

The reply was slow in coming, almost as if the words threatened to choke him. "I already did—once a long time ago. Her name was Beatrice." He was silent for several moments, as if lost in thought, then he cleared his throat. "The lady chose another—one with wealth to go with his title. Now, I no longer believe in love."

Having said this, Paul Clement reached into his tunic again and produced a second letter. This missive, unlike the one from his father, was not crumpled. It was also unopened. He looked from the discreet dark green sealing wafer on the back of the folded vellum to the neat handwriting on the front. "At least," he said, his tone filled with contempt, "the female knows how to write."

Stephen clamped his teeth together to keep from giving voice to his indignation on the young woman's behalf. He and Paul Clement were not friends. They had met at Oxford, where they had attended a few of the same classes, but only their chance meeting this past year as fellow officers had fostered a sort of bond between them. The baronet's son was prideful to a fault, and sometimes Stephen had difficulty ignoring the fellow's exaggerated belief in his own importance. It was that sense of superiority that kept their relationship from being one of real friendship.

When his thoughts returned to the letter writer, a question formed in Stephen's mind: Was Paul Clement prepared to show a wool merchant's daughter the respect and consideration she deserved as a human being? The question might need asking, but Stephen drew the line at such interference.

Apparently the lieutenant felt the major's reticence, but misunderstanding it, he said, "Lest you think I have been sold cheaply, allow me to inform you that the young woman will bring to the marriage a portion in excess of twenty thousand pounds."

"And that is enough? Even if you should take Miss Maitland in dislike?"

"For such a sum as that, believe me, I shall not take her in dislike." He paused a moment, as if reconsidering his answer. "Of course, there are always those little gaucheries that prevail among the lower classes, but I am prepared to overlook such failings. At least for a time. If she is too *outre*, I feel certain I may depend upon my mother to do all within her power to bring her into line."

Again, Stephen kept his tongue between his teeth, but he was beginning to feel a real sympathy for the unsuspecting Miss Maitland. "I see you have not read the letter."

"I have not. Actually, I have been toying with the idea of tossing it, unread, into the fire. Though I am relieved to know my future bride is not illiterate, it would have been better—more ladylike—had she waited until after the engagement became official to begin a correspondence."

"Surely you are being overly nice in your notions. Perhaps Miss Maitland merely wished to extend the hand of friendship. I see nothing amiss in her telling you a little about herself and perhaps asking a question or two of you." Having said this much, Stephen decided to give his opinion of the lieutenant's unyielding attitude regarding the letter. "You are being unconscionably toplofty, and I believe the young woman deserves the courtesy of a reply. It is the least a *gentleman* would do."

At the rebuke, the lieutenant's gray eyes darkened with anger and his hands balled into fists, and for just a moment Stephen thought the smaller man meant to try his luck at landing him a facer. "I would not advise it," he cautioned quietly.

The calmness of his voice did not lessen in any way the very real threat, and the atmosphere inside the tent grew suddenly tense. All was quiet, save for the snores of the two men on their cots, and in the hush, Lieutenant Clement muttered an obscenity.

After relaxing his fists, he ran his hands through his blond locks, then he shrugged as if the contretemps had been nothing more than a simple difference of opinion. "No need to take me to task, old fellow. We have been acquainted for too many years to start fighting now. Besides, if you feel so strongly about the need to reply to the blasted letter, there is a solution."

A smile lit his handsome face, and he lifted the missive and slipped it into the deck of cards Stephen still held. "Since you never receive any communications by post, while I am in possession of a veritable glut of letters, pray allow me to share. The missive is all yours. You may answer the wool merchant's daughter or not. Suit yourself. As for me, I wash my hands of the entire matter."

Chapter One

Plemstock, Oxfordshire, May 1816 . . .

"Cousin Lorna," young Thomas Whidby called, running toward her, waving a letter above his head. "The post has come, and you have got another letter from—"

"Stop!" ordered a feminine voice. "Do not move."

The lad obeyed instantly, though excitement widened his pale blue eyes as he stared at the apparition—an apparition whose head and shoulders were swathed by a heavy gray veil, and whose body was protected by an ankle-length smock secured with draw strings at the neck, sleeves, and hem. In her thickly gloved hand the specter carried a small vial covered over by cheesecloth, and it was to the vial that the ten-year-old boy's attention was drawn.

"Is it the old queen?" he asked, his voice just above a whisper. "I did not know you were moving her today. Has one of the new queens matured enough to become a threat to—"

"Shh," Lorna Maitland replied, her own voice hushed and deliberate. "I pumped smoke into the hive so the worker bees would put their heads into the honeycomb, but the wind has picked up and is dispelling the smoke faster than I can move the queen. If the workers should discover the queen's absence before I have her settled in her new home, you and I will be in for it. You know as well as I do that they will fight to the death to protect her."

The youngster nodded, more intrigued than frightened by the threat of multiple stings.

As Lorna moved toward the newly built skep—a large, domed hive made of twisted straw—she passed the boy, who watched her every movement, his lower lip caught between his teeth to inhibit any words that might attempt to slip out. His freckled face was serious, his wheat-colored Whidby hair blowing in the wind. "Be very still," she ordered.

Once Lorna had removed the cheesecloth and placed the uncovered vial near the opening of the skep, she stepped back and took the youngster by the hand. "Come," she said, "the swarm may already have begun, and if you and I are smart, we will play least in sight before it gets here."

Because her words were underscored by a droning sound that grew stronger with each passing moment, she and Thomas fled with all possible speed. Unfortunately, Lorna's progress was hampered by the fact that her skirt was tied around her ankles, but by using a combination of tiny steps and occasional hops, she made it to the safety of the Grange stable, a good quarter of a mile from the apiary with its half dozen skeps.

"Whew!" Thomas said, his breath coming in gasps, "that was close."

"*Much* too close." Lorna gave a squeeze to his hand then released it. "Thank you, Thomas, for your support. Without it, I am persuaded I would have tripped over my own feet. You were very brave to remain by my side."

The boy's usually serious face grew pink with pleasure. "Do you mean it, Cousin? Was I really brave?"

"A veritable hero. I only wish your mother could have seen the way you—"

Though Lorna clamped her mouth shut, the action came too late; the joy had already left Thomas's eyes, replaced by concern. Silently she berated herself for mentioning the beautiful flibbertigibbet who was the lad's mother. At the same time, she cursed Analise Whidby for hurting Thomas by her unexplained and inexcusable absence.

The lovely Analise had always possessed more hair than wit, and if she had ever entertained two sensible thoughts in the same week, the event had escaped the notice of her only remaining relatives. Still, this latest proof of her irresponsibility was unconscionable. A hedgehog made a better parent!

The woman had sent her only child by post from Tunbridge Wells to Plemstock to stay with the Maitlands, who were distant cousins, and the only explanation she had offered for the boy's surprise sojourn was a hastily scribbled note saying she would come soon to reclaim him. That had been three weeks ago, and though Lorna's father had hired a solicitor to inquire after his wife's second cousin by marriage, the fellow's findings had been inconclusive to say the least.

Her rooms at the fashionable watering hole had been let to another family, and no one questioned had any idea where the lovely widow might be. A certain visiting squire's name came up, but he, too, was among the missing.

Lorna wisely kept that particular piece of information to herself and turned the conversation to the boy's reason for coming to find her. After pulling off the sticky glove and dropping it to the ground, she removed the thick veil that protected her face and upper body. "Now," she said, not bothering to disguise the excitement in her voice, "I believe you said someone had fetched the post."

"Yes, Cousin, and there was a letter for you. From

Warwickshire. Pilcher left it in the salver on the table in the vestibule, insisting that you would see it there the moment you came inside, but I knew you would want to have it as soon as possible."

"And you were correct." No point in pretending reserve, for the entire household knew that Lorna had been anxiously awaiting word from her fiancé, who was supposed to have returned from Belgium a full month ago.

The boy still held the missive, and as if aware that he conveyed an item of great importance, he laid the wafer-sealed paper in her outstretched hand. "Finally," she said. "I was beginning to think I was never to hear from Lieutenant Clement again. I feared the betrothal had been broken off and that I was to be the last to know."

"Cousin!" The army-mad youngster would have none of such heresy. With no adult male in his life, except for Lorna's father, who was already in his middle years, Thomas had decided that Paul Clement was a man worthy to be hero-worshiped. "The lieutenant is an officer and a gentleman. He would never go back on his word."

"Of course he would not." Lorna looked into the indignant face of her young cousin, whose blue eyes and blond hair were so much like her own. "Your pardon, Thomas, for giving voice to such a nonsensical notion. I meant it purely in jest."

After tearing open the wafer and scanning the first few lines, however, Lorna's very real doubts returned. The letter was not from Paul.

Thomas, still believing the lieutenant had written, spoke almost as if to himself. "I can guess what it says. The lieutenant has returned at last, and he is asking permission to call upon you. It is just like Cousin Calvin said, 'A fellow who would write a young lady near a dozen letters in less than a year is the sort of fellow who would call on that young lady the moment he set foot off the ship.' ''

Lorna cleared her throat, embarrassed to be reminded of her father's certainty that Paul would let nothing stop him from coming directly to her. "The letter is from Lady Clement. From Paul's mother." She hurried through the brief, though elegantly penned page, then returned to the beginning and read it once again more slowly.

"I am invited to Clement Park," she said, more to herself than to the boy, "to make the acquaintance of my future family." *And my future husband.*

This last she kept to herself. Not for the world would she let anyone see how nervous she was at the thought of finally coming face-to-face with her fiancé. She had hoped their initial meeting might be in private, so they could get through any awkward moments without other people watching and listening. Obviously, that was not to be.

"But what of the lieutenant?" the boy asked. "Does Lady Clement say when she expects him to return?"

Lorna felt the heat of embarrassment in her face. "The lieutenant is even now at Clement Park. It . . . it seems he has been there for the better part of a month."

The boy stared at her, his mouth agape in disbelief. "A month!"

Thomas's reaction to the news was mild compared to the astonishment of Calvin Maitland, who took the lieutenant's failure to apprise them of his arrival as a personal insult. During the next two days, Lorna was treated to tirade after tirade from her father, with each diatribe ending with her parent threatening to call off the betrothal.

Nor did his ire diminish noticeably during their journey from their well-appointed home in Oxfordshire to the ancestral home of the Clement family in Warwickshire. At the last minute Lorna had decided she could not in good conscience leave Thomas behind, so the boy accompanied them, but not even his presence prompted her father to moderate his words.

"It's nothing less than a ploy to put us in our place," he said, raising his voice to be heard above the rattle of the traveling chaise and pair as they passed yet another yeoman farmer tilling the red soil of the English heartland. "I've no love of schemes, and for tuppence I'd tell John Coachman to turn the team around and take us back this instant to the Grange."

Hoping to calm him, Lorna reached out and laid her gloved hand upon her father's arm. "We are almost there, Papa, for I can see the Cotswolds." She pointed toward the foothills in the distance—foothills that spilled gentle and green over Warwickshire's northern border. "Besides, we passed through Beddingford fully twenty minutes ago, and I am persuaded Clement Park must be quite near."

"We can still turn around. Nothing easier. I've but to give the word, and—"

"No, Papa. The time for turning back was yesterday afternoon, when we first set out, *before* we traveled the full fifty-five miles. Now, all I wish for is that the journey will come to an end so that I may forsake the incessant rocking of the coach."

Calvin Maitland clamped his rough workman's hand over his daughter's, squeezing her fine-boned fingers in his usual gruff manner. "I'm a thoughtless old fool, lass. Of course you're tired. And though you've denied it a dozen times since you got that cursed letter, I'll wager your pride has taken a bit of a thrashing."

She cast a meaningful glance toward Thomas, who sat on the forward seat beside him, but her father seemed not to notice. "You're a sensible female," he continued, "and I'm proud to say you don't fly into the boughs over every little thing, but the truth of the matter is, it was an unconscionable slight for her ladyship to wait a full month before inviting you to come to Clement Park. Not but what the lieutenant should have done the writing himself, the moment he returned."

Tired of pretending otherwise, Lorna admitted that it was so. "It was a bit of a disappointment, but—"

"I knew it! You can't pull the wool over Calvin Maitland's eyes, for I know the ways of the—"

"*But*—as I was about to say, Papa—you and I are not privy to the period of adjustment needed by a soldier fresh from the wars. Especially one who has endured a battle as horrible as Waterloo. And for that reason, I have decided not to take offense."

As Lorna spoke, she touched the antique locket she always wore, drawing needed courage from the miniature held within the delicate gold frame. The locket had been her mother's, but the portrait inside was of Paul. Sir Duncan, Paul's father, had sent the small oval by the solicitor who had originally suggested the possibility of an alliance between their two families—an alliance Lorna had at first refused even to consider. Then she had been shown the miniature, and when she looked upon the lieutenant's handsome face, she had begun to rethink her hasty refusal.

After that, of course, the first of the letters had arrived.

Over the past two days, she had drawn strength from rereading each of the ten letters Paul had written her from Belgium, including the very moving one he wrote just after the battle of Waterloo. Rereading those tattered pages had convinced her to reserve

judgment until after she and her fiancé had spoken
face-to-face.

Keeping her thoughts to herself, Lorna touched the
russet brown reticule that matched her faille traveling pelisse; the small stack of letters rested inside the
handbag. The missives were tied with a yellow rib-
bon and wrapped in a fresh linen handkerchief to
keep them safe from harm, for Lorna valued those
pages more than anything else in her possession.

Paul's first letter had been little more than a courtesy reply to her own brief note, a bit stiffly worded
if the truth be told, but his second one had been very
different. Following a battle that must have been the
closest thing to hell upon this earth, he had written
to Lorna, pouring out his heart, holding nothing
back. He had told her of the misery and death all
around him, and of the seeming miles of wounded
and dying soldiers, both British and French. He had
spoken of his anguish at being unable to offer aid or
solace to the dying, and of his anger at the unmitigated stupidity of war.

Lorna had replied to his impassioned words with
what consolation she could offer, quoting to him
from the biblical prophets and from Shakespeare's
sonnets, bidding him, in the Bard's words, "No more
be grieved at that which thou hast done." From that
time their correspondence had changed. In the letters
that followed, it was as though they spoke as old
friends—friends who might say what they felt without fear of being judged and found wanting, friends
who shared many of the same sentiments, even the
same sense of humor.

At some point, after reading his letters so many
times she had them memorized word for word,
Lorna Maitland fell in love with Paul Clement.

"It's because I've all the money," her father said,
bringing his daughter's thoughts back to the present.

"The Clement family is centuries old, and they take great pride in their ancestry. And though Sir Duncan is only a baronet, they're accepted everywhere in the land. Still, these days money speaks with a powerful voice, and well Sir Duncan knows it. And that's why they've offered us this insult, to put us in our place, so to speak. They don't want us to be forgetting that they are the Clements, and that we're no but a wool merchant and his daughter."

"But, Papa, that is what we are, and I do not choose to forget it. Nor do I make any apologies for it. I am, and always have been, proud to be the daughter of Calvin Maitland, a man who is respected from one end of England to the other. You are a good man. Honest and genuinely kind, a man who—"

"Hush, now, lass, there's a good girl. Ye've no need ter put me ter the blush in front of young Thomas."

Since her father's complexion was always red, as a result of a childhood spent laboring in the fields, it would have been difficult to detect a blush, but Lorna knew from the sudden return of his thick, Western Derbyshire accent that he was moved by her fervent defense of him. He was everything she had said—a good and honest man—and, as any who did business with him could attest, he was especially shrewd when it came to reading people's motives. Still, she prayed his suspicions about the Clement family would prove groundless, and that this was not some bid for control on their part.

Lorna had hoped Paul's family would like her immediately and welcome her into their midst, but if they did not, she was willing to give them time to grow accustomed to her. Under no circumstances, however, would she tolerate any snubbing of her beloved father.

"And it's not, after all," Calvin Maitland said, returning to the subject of the perceived slight, "as though you've none but sheepherders as your forebears. Your mother, God rest her soul, was a Whidby."

"I am a Whidby," Thomas said, adding his mite to the conversation.

"That you are, lad, and don't you forget it, for your greatgrandda and Lorna's was an admiral in His Majesty's Navy."

"My father was in the navy too," the boy added. "He was a hero."

"True enough," he replied, though with less enthusiasm. "Your da stood shoulder to shoulder with Nelson at Trafalgar and held the admiral's hand as he breathed his last. Now there was a true hero if ever there was one."

Genuinely fond of the lad, Calvin Maitland couched his words in such a way that his young auditor never suspected the hero to whom he referred was Horatio Nelson. As for the thirty-five-year-old Ensign Whidby, that foolish gentleman survived the battle of Trafalgar only to die of influenza the following year—influenza he contracted while escorting his pretty seventeen-year-old bride to the endless round of parties given during the season in London.

Since that piece of information had never been revealed to the boy, the lad sighed with pleasure, always happy to have someone speak of the father he never knew. "My grandfather Whidby was first cousin to Cousin Lorna's grandfather, and I look just like him."

"Aye, lad, that you do. Both you and Lorna have the Whidby looks."

Calvin Maitland returned his attention to his daughter. "I've just one more thing to say, lass, and

I want you to remember it. Margery Whidby may have married beneath her when she gave her hand to a Maitland, but Paul Clement has no reason to say the same. You're as suitable to be the next Lady Clement as any female in the land.''

To Lorna's relief, the coachman turned the horses onto a private carriage drive that sloped downward slightly, and her father abandoned the subject of his daughter's pedigree in favor of hanging out the window so he might get his first glimpse of Clement Park. ''It's impressive,'' he said, as though Lorna could not see the handsome Tudor manor house for herself, its marblestone glowing warm and pink in the late morning sunshine.

''And big,'' Thomas added from his position hanging out the other window.

The house sat in a hollow of the hills of the Cotswold Edge, and though Warwickshire was a county comprised mostly of farmlands and woods, Clement Park did not appear out of place. In fact, it perfectly suited its setting, and when Lorna muttered a rather breathless ''Oh,'' she decided her reaction was forgivably human.

Several months ago she had purchased a guidebook of the area, so she was aware that the construction of the house was begun in the latter part of the fifteenth century and that it took forty years to complete. What she had not been prepared for was the magnificence of the place.

The author of the book had rhapsodized for a full three pages over the rich topiary, the battlement-type turrets, and the moat that had been filled in during the seventeenth century, leaving two charming fish ponds from that era. Even so, the author's descriptions had not done justice to the house or to the park.

Paul Clement's home was simply the most beautiful place Lorna had ever beheld. And soon it would be her home as well.

"It's a showy pile of rocks and mortar," her father said, effectively spoiling the enchanted moment for her. "No wonder the family has outrun their money, for that barn of a place must require more servants than your Cousin Thomas has freckles."

"Papa!"

"Truth is truth, lass. Come winter, I'll wager those tall windows that line the front of the place will let in the cold gusts something fierce. Furthermore, if I know aught of these old houses, there'll not be a single chimney that draws properly. If you'll take my advice, you'll see you have plenty of good wool frocks to keep you warm."

As the carriage rattled over the limestone bridge that separated the ponds, her father finally got his fill of gawking at her future home and sat back against the squabs. "It's right splendid," he said, "but I'd not choose it over our own home. Epping Grange may be little more than fifty years old, and its sturdy brick and flint not nearly so elegant as that pink marblestone, but I believe I prefer it for all that. There's something to be said for having all the modern conveniences. A cozy fire in the—"

"Good day to you, youngster," someone said from outside the coach. At the sound of the deep voice, Calvin Maitland was surprised into silence.

"Good day, sir," Thomas replied.

Father and daughter both turned to stare past the boy, who still hung out the coach window. A horse and rider had drawn up alongside the chaise, and they were keeping pace with the slow-moving vehicle.

"I trust you had a good trip," the rider said.

"*I* did," the boy confided. "We came fifty-five miles, and though I could travel twice that amount without being tired, my Cousin Lorna is heartily sick of the incessant rocking of the coach."

"Thomas!" Lorna whispered, hoping to stop the boy before he said anything more. "Sit back, if you please." To her dismay, he appeared to be far too interested in the horse and rider to heed her softly spoken words.

Apparently the rider's hearing was more acute, for a smile pulled at the corners of his mouth. "If such a distance tired her, I must assume your cousin is quite an *elderly* lady."

"Oh, yes, sir. Five-and-twenty, I think."

"Thomas!"

The man chuckled, and though he could not possibly see inside the coach, he tipped his curly brimmed beaver. "Good day, ma'am. If you are Miss Lorna Maitland, allow me to tell you how pleased I am to make your acquaintance at last."

Chapter Two

*A*t *last?* What could he mean by such a remark?
Far too startled to reply to the man's puzzling
greeting, Lorna drew back against the squabs. While
she attempted to make herself invisible, her father
sat forward so he might steal a look at the speaker.

A smile lit the middle-aged man's face. "I knew
it!" he said, his tone for once held to a whisper. "It's
the lieutenant come to meet us. Now there's a good
sign, lass. Not but what it's just as it should be, for
what young gentleman would not be eager to meet
his fiancée? None, I'll wager, and I like Paul Clement
the more for his eagerness."

Lorna still said nothing. Embarrassment held her
silent, else she could have told her father that the
rider was not her fiancé. From the elegant cut of the
man's clothes, and the beauty of the spirited gray
gelding he rode, the fellow was obviously a gentleman, but he was not Paul Clement. Even if he had
not removed his hat to reveal dark, thick hair, Lorna
would have known he was not the man she most
wanted to see.

Paul was a modern-day Adonis—fair and slender,
with an elegant, almost beautiful profile—the very
antithesis of the man before them. This man's hair
and eyes were only slightly darker than his complexion, which had been turned a coppery hue by the

sun, and his face was too rugged, his jaw too stubborn for any pretensions to male beauty.

Furthermore, where Paul was almost otherworldly, putting one in mind of the romantic poets, this man was tall and broad-shouldered and all too real. Though he appeared unaware of the fact that he positively exuded vitality and strength, Lorna could feel those qualities from several feet away. For some reason, the experience left her feeling a bit breathless.

Judging by the smile upon her father's face, and the unallayed awe upon Thomas's freckled visage, the rider was the kind of man that other males admired. As for his effect upon the female sex, Lorna would not let herself even consider the matter—especially since there was about the man a certain dangerous quality that sent a disquieting shiver up her spine.

Whoever he was, she wished he would ride on. She did not like her reaction to him, and she definitely did not wish to make his acquaintance. His very presence was unsettling, and Lorna thanked heaven that she was engaged to Paul Clement and not to this dark, disturbingly masculine stranger.

"You sit a horse like an cavalryman," Thomas said, respect in his voice. "Are you Lieutenant Clement? Are you my cousin's fiancé?"

"I am a soldier," he replied, "or more accurately, I *was* a soldier. However, I am not Clement. Like you, I am but a visitor here." He inclined his head in an abbreviated bow. "I am Major Stephen Rutledge, at your service."

Much to Lorna's relief, before anything more could be said, the coachman yelled a loud "Whoa," then reined in the team beside a wide covered portico. Thankfully, the major was obliged to move aside or risk injury to his mount, and in the ensuing bustle of servants coming to help them alight then whisk them inside, Lorna was able to avoid looking in the man's direction.

She still had not the least notion what he had meant by saying he was pleased to meet her *at last*? To her certain knowledge, she had never even heard of Major Stephen Rutledge.

As it happened, the gentleman's very existence was expunged from Lorna's thoughts the instant she entered the house. And no wonder! It was, indeed, a grand establishment.

She was not alone in her opinion; her father stared in awe at the dauntingly large vestibule. "Blimey!" he said.

Silently Lorna agreed with him, for the damask-covered room rose the full three stories of the house, with nothing to soften the overpowering walls save the polished oak balcony that divided them horizontally and gave access to all of the rooms on the first floor. Several marble statues filled the niches in the lower walls of the cavernous room, and Lorna would have liked to look her fill of them. Regrettably, that activity was denied her. In fact, she was not even given a moment to remove her bonnet and make herself presentable before a rather pompous butler ushered the threesome up the stairs.

"Her ladyship is waiting," he said, his tone one of undisguised reproach.

"Eh, what's this?" Calvin Maitland said. "Are we not to be shown to our rooms?"

"This way," the butler said, leading them toward the drawing room, where the family waited. Like tardy students, they were hurried along half the length of the balcony, their footfalls echoing in the vast space, and only when the butler reached the door of an apartment he had termed the blue withdrawing room did he pause.

While Lorna strove to catch her breath, the servant

threw open the door to a formal room, large and rectangular, decorated in shades of blue and silver. "Miss Maitland," he announced to the middle-aged couple who sat on opposite sides of the oversized marble fireplace. "And Mr. Maitland," he added, his tone exhibiting not a hint of interest, "also Master Whidby."

"Excellent!" said the gentleman who stood at their entrance. He crossed the room with a confidence that seemed to speak of past generations of Clements—generations who knew their place in the world and drew immense pride from the knowledge. He came directly to Lorna. "You are come at last, my dear Miss Maitland. How do you do? I am Duncan Clement."

Lorna curtsied to their host. Still handsome, Sir Duncan was the original from which his son had been fashioned. Like Paul, he was quite slender, with a classical profile, and though his blond hair was now liberally sprinkled with silver, his gray eyes were almost identical to the eyes Lorna knew so well from the miniature contained in the antique gold locket she wore around her neck.

"How do you do, sir?" she said, placing her hand in his. "I have looked forward to meeting you."

"Thank you, my dear."

After offering no more than a curt nod in Calvin Maitland's direction, and taking no notice whatever of young Thomas, Sir Duncan led Lorna over to the fireplace, where his wife sat straight and regal in a high-back chair that might almost have been a throne. She was a small woman, but for all her lack of size, she held herself as though she were no less a personage than Queen Charlotte.

"Adele," her husband said, "allow me to present to you your future daughter-in-law. Miss Maitland, this is Lady Clement."

"Miss Maitland," she said, holding out two be-ringed fingers.

Lorna curtsied, then touched the proffered fingers. Like the room, the lady's hand was cool. "Lady Clement," she said. "It was kind of you, ma'am, to invite us to your home."

Adele Clement was younger than Lorna had expected, perhaps not yet fifty, with light brown hair and blue eyes, and though her bone structure was delicate, anyone mistaking her for a fragile female had only to match their gaze with hers. Admirals and Iron Dukes should possess such piercing eyes!

In one swift glance her ladyship took the younger woman's measure. The result of that assessment Lorna was not to know, for Sir Duncan reclaimed her attention immediately.

"Of course," he said, touching her elbow so he might turn her toward the far end of the room, "you will want to say a word to my son. Paul, make your bow to your fiancée."

Paul is here!

Lorna had not realized that anyone else was in the room, and just knowing that the man she loved was but a few feet away caused her heart to beat painfully against her ribs and her knees to quake as though they were formed from India rubber.

Of course, this was not the way Lorna had dreamed of meeting her future husband. She had wanted their first moments together to be romantic and memorable. Instead, the suddenness of the encounter made her feel nervous and not a little gauche. Now, as she allowed Sir Duncan to turn her toward his son, she prayed she would not trip over her own feet, or that she would not utter an inane remark, like some empty-headed widgeon. Fortunately, all thoughts of herself vanished the instant she beheld Paul Clement.

Her first sight of her fiancé nearly stole her breath away, for he was even more beautiful than the likeness in the miniature. He stood before a pair of long windows at the top of the room, and the afternoon sunlight that shone through the lace curtains behind him created a sort of aura, making him appear almost ethereal. With the light beaming upon Paul's blond head, he put Lorna in mind of one of Botticelli's angels.

"How do you do?" he said, making her a graceful bow.

Lorna felt as if she had been turned to stone. The moment she had imagined thousands of times had finally arrived, and she could not move. Nor could she seem to find her voice. Only when this heavenly vision came toward her was she finally able to make a sound. "How do you do," she said, stammering like some schoolroom chit.

If their meeting caused a similar nervousness in her fiancé, he hid it well. As he held out his hand to her, he appeared perfectly calm—the word *dispassionate* flitted across Lorna's brain, but she dismissed it immediately. When she placed her hand in his, he bowed over her fingers, lightly brushing them with his lips. His lips were cold upon her skin, so cold that Lorna had to stop herself from snatching her hand away.

Thankfully, she was saved from committing such a missish act by the recollection of a line from one of Paul's letters. At the time, she had thought the words pure poetry.

Sunlight, I regret to say that I have taken it for granted. After the cold, ugly realities of war, I shall never do so again. Indeed, I shall treasure the sun's warmth more than gold.

Remembering that letter enabled Lorna to relax. "Were you treasuring the sunlight?"

He gave her a blank stare. "What?"

"The sunlight," she repeated. "You wrote of it in one of your letters."

"Oh, yes. Quite."

An awkward silence followed his response, and Lorna was almost relieved when she heard the door open and someone enter the room. The newcomer was not announced, but even though Lorna did not turn around immediately to look at him, she knew who it was. She felt his energy bring instant life to the chilly room.

"Major," Thomas said, the relief in his boyish voice echoing the sigh emitted by Calvin Maitland. "Good day, sir."

"Bantling," Stephen Rutledge said. After giving the boy's shoulder a squeeze, he offered his hand to Lorna's father. "How do you do, Mr. Maitland?"

"I do well enough," he replied, taking the major's hand and giving it a hearty shake. "Thank ye for asking," he added, his meaning not lost on his daughter, who blushed for the thoughtlessness of her future family.

"This is a pleasure," the major continued, "for I understand, Mr. Maitland, that you and I have something in common."

"Have we noo? And what might that be?"

"We are fellow Derbyshire men. It has been more than ten years since I left Hatton, but I have fond memories of the place. While you are here, sir, I hope you will not mind telling me how the county has grown since last I saw it."

"Not at all, Major. Like nothing better. But first you must tell me how it is you knew that I was from Derbyshire."

Stephen Rutledge's dark eyes lit with merriment,

and he put his tongue in his cheek. "Nay, sir," he said, "I'll no tell. Tha's for ye ter discover."

The younger man's accent was such a perfect imitation of her father's that Lorna was hard pressed not to laugh, and she realized that this was the first time since she arrived at Clement Park that she had been tempted even to smile.

Her father laughed aloud. "You're an impudent dog, Major, and I'll thank you to show a bit of respect for your elders."

Above the laughter, Paul spoke, though his comment was addressed to no one in particular. "Stephen makes a joke of everything. He takes getting used to."

An awkward silence followed the remark, and while a red-faced Sir Duncan hurried to introduce Calvin Maitland to Lady Clement, the major crossed the room to join his fellow officer and Lorna. Though she was grateful to Stephen Rutledge for his show of good manners toward her father and Thomas, she wished he had remained with them.

She wanted a few minutes privacy with Paul. She had barely exchanged a dozen words with her fiancé, and in a house as large as this, who could tell when they might have the opportunity for another moment of private conversation.

"May we meet later?" she whispered. "When we drove up the carriageway, I thought I spied a garden to the right of the house. Perhaps you would show it to me?"

"Of course," Paul replied. "If that is your wish."

If his response bore little resemblance to that expected of a supposedly eager lover, Lorna credited his seeming disinterest to the fact that his friend was within hearing distance.

As Stephen approached Paul Clement and the wool merchant's daughter, he took a moment to study the young lady. Even allowing for her trim figure and the combination of silky blond hair and sky blue eyes, Miss Lorna Maitland was not a true beauty, at least, not by fashionable standards. There was, however, something about her that drew one's attention—a certain liveliness of expression that Stephen found most pleasing. He thought he had seen her biting back a smile when he teased her father, and he made it his mission to see if he could get a genuine laugh from her.

After making her a bow, he said, "Your servant, Miss Maitland. I understand that you found the rigors of the journey here wearying."

The look she gave him said he would do well to leave that subject alone. Naturally, he did not do so. " 'Twas no doubt a touch of rheumatism brought on by your advanced years."

The merest hint of a smile teased her lips. "No doubt."

"We must hope, ma'am, that you have recovered your strength by Thursday. Is three days sufficient, do you think?"

The lady was obliged to press her lips together to keep them still, but she could not hide the amusement in her eyes. It was as Stephen suspected, laughter was the making of her. With but an upward tilt of her mouth, Miss Lorna Maitland was transformed from merely pretty to quite lovely.

"I should think," she replied, "that three days would be adequate for the restoration of even the most enfeebled constitution. Am I to assume that another journey is planned—one in which I am to take an active part?"

"Only a very short journey, ma'am. Your fiancé and I thought you might enjoy a visit to Stratford-upon-Avon."

She turned to Paul Clement then, bestowing upon

him a smile of such warmth that it should have prompted any red-blooded man to whisk her off with unseemly haste to some secluded spot. "I should enjoy it of all things," she said, her voice slightly breathless. "How kind of you, Paul, to think of it."

If Clement had ever possessed a drop of red blood, he had obviously lost it, for he did not even return her smile. "It was Stephen's idea," he said. "For some reason, he was convinced you would wish to see Mr. Shakespeare's home, and I have no objections to a ride about the neighborhood."

"I . . . I see." When the lady turned back to Stephen, the spontaneous smile had been replaced by one of mere politeness. "How is it, Major, that you guessed my partiality for Shakespeare? Did my accent give me away?"

Good for her! The lady had spunk.

"No, ma'am. As far as I can tell, you have no accent. My assumption was based purely upon your sex. I have yet to meet a lady who does not enjoy Shakespeare's sonnets. And if I know anything of the matter, you will have set at least one of them to memory. Tell us, Miss Maitland, which is your favorite?"

"I should be hard pressed to choose only one, sir, After all, each sonnet is beautiful in its own way. However, I admit to a partiality for—"

"I have no particular liking for poetry," Paul informed her. "And I hope, Miss Maitland, that you are not one of those idle creatures who sits about forever lost in a book."

Surprise and embarrassment warred for prominence on the lady's face, but before she could speak, her young cousin jumped into the breach. "Cousin Lorna is not idle," he said, his tone defensive. "People come to her all the time for help, and she always—"

"Thomas, please. I am persuaded Lieutenant Clement meant no—"

"Furthermore," the boy added with pride, "she keeps bees."

A smothered gasp came from the far side of the room.

"My cousin knows everything there is to know about bees and about gathering honey, and she helps the tenants start their own apiaries so they can earn extra money to feed their fam—"

"Thomas!" This time his cousin's tone brooked no disobedience. "Come here, if you please, and look at the view from this window. I believe I see a small stream meandering in the distance."

While the boy did as he was bid and joined the young lady at the window, Stephen spoke softly to Paul. "Give over, old fellow. Surely a person may enjoy a bit of reading without it condemning him— or her—as a layabout."

"As the future Lady Clement," Paul replied, not bothering to lower his voice, "much will be expected of her."

Though the lady in question pretended an interest in the view, Stephen felt certain she had heard their exchange. Hoping to put an end to the conversation, he said, "I am confident that a young woman of Miss Maitland's resourcefulness will be up to any task."

Unfortunately, Paul did not take the hint, but continued with his line of thought. "She will, of course, look to my mother for guidance. Mother will know how to instruct her both in her duties as my wife and in those little rules of ladylike deportment that may not previously have come in her way."

Stephen detected a flash of rebellion in the young lady's eyes, as if she were about to protest such autocratic behavior on the part of her betrothed. If such was her design, the moment was lost when Lady

Clement claimed everyone's attention by instructing her husband to ring the bell for the butler. "It is time," she said, "that our guests be shown to their rooms."

Within a matter of minutes, the wool merchant, his daughter, and their young relative were being invited to follow the servant to the west wing. Before they quit the room, however, the young lady said something to her fiancé, and whatever the whispered message, it was apparently meant for his ears alone.

"There are things we must discuss," Lorna had whispered to Paul just before she left the blue drawing room. "Please meet me in the garden in an hour."

"I will try," he had answered, and with that unloverlike response Lorna was obliged to be content.

Now, while she waited for her fiancé to come to her, she sat on an unforgiving stone bench and looked about her in disappointment at the garden. She would not have believed it possible, but the long, narrow yew-enclosed expanse held absolutely no charm.

The past winter had been one of the coldest in history, and the spring seemed to be waiting for some moment in the future to make an appearance, so the flowers were late in blooming. Still, it was not the sparseness of the garden that robbed it of appeal. Every rosebush and each bed of flowers—the asphodels, the larkspur, and even the golden iris—were so precisely planted and so meticulously pruned that they had lost every last ounce of beauty and spontaneity.

Soon growing bored with the too-perfect garden, where not even a bee buzzed its way about the flowers, Lorna had little to occupy her thoughts but Paul's rather cavalier offer to "try" to meet her. She cautioned herself not to take umbrage at his reply, nor to read more into it than was probably meant, and yet, when the designated hour was accomplished then exceeded by an additional fifteen minutes, and Paul had not arrived, it was difficult not to take offense. While she waited, it was equally difficult not to remember their first meeting and Paul's unmistakable coolness toward her.

Was it shyness that had prompted such reserve in his manner? Lorna sincerely hoped that was the case, for it would explain much. Judging by his letters, however, a person would never suspect that Paul suffered from shyness. Far from it.

Without really knowing why, Lorna had always pictured him as a born leader, the kind of man to whom others turned for help or advice or just a cheery word. Such men are not usually timid, but then, she could be mistaken. After all, she knew very little of the ways of gentlemen.

In the small village of Plemstock, where she had lived her entire twenty-five years, there were few eligible men between the ages of sixteen and forty, and of those few, none were disposed to pursue the wool merchant's daughter. As for the men she met when traveling to one or other of the spa towns, experience had taught Lorna to avoid those would-be suitors.

Calvin Maitland and his daughter did not move in the first circles of society, and Lorna had learned early on that most of the men who pursued her had one of two objectives in mind. Either they were sporting gentlemen who had gambled away their family fortunes and were hanging out for a rich wife—no matter her age, looks, or amiability—or they were enterprising clerks who wanted to use an acquaintance with Lorna as a means of meeting and doing business with her father. Whatever their motives, Lorna spurned their overtures.

It was those circumstances that had prompted Calvin Maitland to take seriously Sir Duncan's suggestion of an alliance between their two families.

Her father wanted grandchildren, but most of all he wished his daughter to know the joy of a home and a family of her own. Lorna shared his ambition for her; otherwise, she never would have taken her first look at the miniature of Paul Clement. Still, her dreams included something more than just a home and children; she desperately wanted love to be a part of the experience.

Hoping the miniature would work its usual magic, she removed her bonnet, lifted the gold chain over her head, then opened the delicate locket to look at the face of her fiancé. After a few moments of quiet reflection, she sighed. "Yes," she said, "you are still the man I love."

Her qualms calmed by the portrait, Lorna reminded herself of what she had told her father about a returning soldier needing time before resuming his old life. If that was true, it was also possible that the soldier might need time before stepping into a *new* life.

Closing her eyes, she called to mind the last letter she had received from Paul, a brief note penned shortly before he was to return to England.

My friend, this may be my last letter to you. Once I am back on English soil, the change in our circumstances will alter our present relationship. From that time, nothing will ever be the same, and I shall miss you more than I can say. Thank you for your letters. They saved my sanity.

He had signed the missive, *Your friend,* just as he always did, for he never used either her name or his own. At the time it had seemed perfectly natural, and by her third letter to him, Lorna had followed his lead, dispensing with names as well.

"Was your assessment correct?" she asked the portrait. "Has your coming home changed everything? Do you now wish the engagement at an end?"

She was still pondering that question when she heard footfalls on the crushed-stone path. Delighted that he had come at last, she smiled and turned to greet her betrothed. The smile was short lived, for the man who walked toward her, his stride graceful and assured, was not Paul.

"You!" she said, unable to hide the disappointment in her voice. "What do you want?"

Chapter Three

"My, my," Stephen Rutledge said, continuing toward her. "If it were morning, Miss Maitland, and not late afternoon, I might suppose you had gotten up on the wrong side of the bed. Am I to gather from your apparent displeasure at seeing me that you were expecting someone else?"

Lorna snapped shut the locket, slipped the chain back over her head, and let the antique gold circle fall against her bosom. She knew she should apologize to the major for her rudeness, but somehow she could not. His presence was unsettling, and for the life of her she could not understand why it should be so.

"I *was* expecting someone, sir, and I would appreciate it if you would choose some other place for your walk."

The man was obviously immune to rudeness, for his mouth twitched just the slightest bit at the corners, as though he were trying to contain a smile, and though she found his amusement irritating in the extreme, her attention was caught by his firm lips. They were well shaped and perfectly suited to his dark, rugged visage, but they were not the lips Lorna had been waiting more than an hour to see.

Not lips! she corrected herself, *face.* His was not the *face* she had been waiting to see.

Already annoyed with herself for that mental slip

of the tongue, Lorna was vexed even further when the interloper had the effrontery to sit down beside her, though he was unwanted and most definitely uninvited.

"Major Rutledge," she said, moving to the edge of the bench and snatching at her skirt so it was no longer caught beneath his muscular thigh, "you prompt me to rudeness, for—"

"Be as rude as you like," he invited, his tone so relaxed and affable an eavesdropper might be forgiven for thinking them old friends. "I make it a policy never to take offense when I am in a sunny garden with a pretty lady."

Lorna sat very straight, hoping her unwelcoming posture would depress further familiarity. "Save your compliments for someone who might welcome them, Major. I do not."

His dark eyebrows lifted in spurious surprise. "Surely you did not think *that* a compliment?"

Embarrassed now, Lorna stammered over an apology. "I thought . . . that is to say—"

"If I had meant to compliment you, madam, I would have been more specific. For instance, I would have mentioned something about—"

"I assure you, sir, an example is not at all necessary."

"About your hair," he continued, as though she had not spoken. "When I first spied you sitting here in the garden, I thought perhaps one of Shakespeare's fairies had sprinkled their dust over me, for the scene was one of magic."

Lorna told herself to turn away, not to listen to this stranger, yet for some reason she paid no heed to her own advice.

"Pure magic," he repeated, "for amid the flowers sat a lovely lady quite deep in thought, and while she contemplated what appeared to be a miniature in a locket, the sun's rays sat softly upon her hair, turning the silken strands the color of warmed wheat." He leaned toward her an inch or so and breathed deeply, as if he might capture the nutlike fragrance of that sun-warmed edible. "Ummm," he said, his voice soft and low, "very nice."

Somehow Lorna resisted the temptation to reach up and touch her hair. If the truth be told, the only warmth she felt seemed to be stealing up her spine, and the sensation was decidedly tingly. "Sir, you pass the line of what is pleasing. I am an engaged woman, and as such—"

"I am aware of your betrothal, ma'am. That is why, as a gentleman, I refrained from remarking upon the color of your eyes."

There was that tingly feeling again, and Lorna only just stopped herself from asking him what remark he might have made. Apparently he needed no encouragement, for he said, "The blue puts me in mind of some wildflowers I saw growing on a rocky hillside just outside Brussels. Gentians, I believe they were called."

Gentians. Lorna lowered her gaze, and for several seconds she concentrated upon the bonnet in her lap. With the best will in the world, however, she could not stop herself from looking up at him once again. "You could not know it, sir, but gentians are my favorite flower."

He studied a minuscule piece of lint on his sleeve. "Are they now?"

As if only just noticing the formality of the garden, he said, "Unlike this lot, the gentian is an unpretentious flower. Those in Belgium were clear and fresh as only nature could plant them. Their leaves were boxlike and a yellowish green, with little tufts of dense foliage growing upon the small stems, and out of that foliage arose flowers of a breathtaking, iridescent blue. A blue so like your eyes that when you first looked up at me, I fancied myself back on that hillside."

Iridescent? Breathtaking? Lorna felt a certain breathlessness herself. Thankfully, she was not obliged to speak, for it appeared the major had not finished with his reminiscences.

"I discovered that quiet hillside just a day or two before the battles began. Many a night," he added, his voice no longer teasing, "I clung to the memory of those gentians. They were like a lovely talisman amid the ugliness of war."

Recalling that Stephen Rutledge had only just returned from the horrors of Waterloo, Lorna experienced a fellow-feeling so strong and so achingly familiar that she reached out and laid her hand upon his sleeve.

He looked at her hand, then without a word he captured her fingers in his strong grasp, held them for a moment, then slowly raised them to his lips.

The major's lips were firm and warm, and the touch of them against Lorna's skin did strange things to her senses, making her wonder how those lips would feel against her own. The moment seemed to go on forever, as if suspended in time, and all was quiet save for the soft, melodious song of a chiff chaff perched on a rose trellis near the bottom of the garden.

"You cannot do it," he said, the words so soft Lorna almost did not hear them.

She had no idea what he meant by those whispered words, and still a bit bemused by the image of the major's mouth capturing hers, she was obliged to call herself back to the moment. "What can I not do?"

"You cannot marry Paul Clement."

Reality was like a face full of cold water. "What?"

"You and Paul are strangers, and—"

"Sir," she said, snatching her hand from his. "This is none of your affair, and I will thank you to keep your opinions to yourself."

Stephen allowed her to reclaim her hand, but he could not do as she asked—he could not remain silent. "You are an intelligent woman. Surely it needed only a matter of minutes in their company for you to see that you will never belong in that family."

She stiffened. "Sir, you are impertinent. I only just met Sir Duncan and Lady Clement, but I am persuaded they are a—"

"Pair of cold fish," he finished for her.

"Do not put words in my mouth, Major. I had meant to say that they are everything that is amiable."

"Liar."

"Major Rutledge!"

"And what of your fiancée? Do not bother telling me that you thought him amiable as well, for I will not believe you. I saw your face when he decreed that his mother should furnish you with instruction on the subject of ladylike behavior."

"You . . . you goaded him into saying it."

Stephen shook his head. "I had no part in his remarks. Clement voiced only what he believes to be true."

Observing her growing anger, Stephen feared his words had fallen upon deaf ears.

"It is clear," she said, "that you do not wish to see Paul and me wed."

"Acquit me of that, at least. I did not come to Warwickshire to put a stumbling block in the way of this betrothal, I merely wished to satisfy myself that you were truly—"

"Say no more," she said, holding her hand up for silence. "It is obvious that you came to satisfy your-

self that the wool merchant's daughter was suitable
to marry your friend."

"Not at all. Now it is *you* who are putting words
in *my* mouth."

She stood then, her head high and her chin reso-
lute. "Believe me, sir, I understand your wish to protect your friend. After all, you and he have been
through a war together. Such experiences, I am told,
forge a bond between people. Still, it would have
been fairer to Paul, and to me, if you had waited at
least five minutes before you drew your conclusions.
Who knows, Major, if you had withheld your judgment until I had been here a day or two, you might
even have come to like me."

"You mistake me, Miss Maitland. The friend I
came here to protect is—"

"Cousin Lorna! Where are you, Cousin?"

"Here, Thomas," she called to the youngster who
had just turned the corner of the garden.

The boy ran toward them, his feet setting small
pieces of gravel flying. "Cousin," he began without
preamble, "must I remain in the nursery, like some
little boy? Simmons, that pickle-faced butler says I
am not to leave the upper floor, lest I knock over a
vase or something."

The lady stepped away from the stone bench,
using the boy's arrival to put distance between herself and Stephen. "Did you knock over a vase?"
she asked.

Thomas pulled himself erect, as if affronted by the
question. "No such of a thing!"

"Then what was it?" Her tone was quiet but firm,
and faced with an authority he obviously respected,
the lad sighed, relaxing his offended pose.

"It was only a small writing slate, and not even a
new one at that. Honest, Cousin. And though I assured the maid they sent to watch my every move

that I would pay for the slate, she reported the incident to the butler all the same."

"A slate?" Miss Maitland asked calmly. "Nothing more?" At his nod, she said, "I do not think that such a great crime. Before we leave, we will go to the village, where you may purchase a replacement. With your own money, of course, so you will remember to be more careful in the future."

Stephen would not have been surprised to hear a bit of argument from the boy about the disbursement of his own funds; after all, youngsters' pockets were always to let, but the lad merely exhaled loudly, as if happy to be reassured that his family was on his side. Then, the matter obviously banished from his mind, he said, "Cousin, you wouldn't believe the way they keep the nursery, with every toy and book arranged just so on the shelves, as if they were not to be touched."

"It sounds rather forbidding," Stephen said.

The lady kept her back to him, as if to demonstrate her total lack of interest in his opinion; instead, she spoke to the boy. "Surely you realize, Thomas, that the apartment has not been used in years."

"Yes, ma'am, but it is more than that. It is like a museum or something up there. Totally uninviting. I pity any boy or girl who has to grow up there."

"Out of the mouths of babes," Stephen said.

Young Thomas gave him an impudent smile, but the lady chose to ignore the remark. She had heard it, though, for she plopped her bonnet atop her head and tied the ribbons, the lopsided bow and overly tight knot giving testimony of her anger. "Come," she said, putting her arm around the boy's shoulder and turning him in the direction from which he had just come, "let us see if we can find that stream we saw from the drawing room window. I am persuaded that you and I would benefit from a bit of exercise before returning to the house."

The youngster allowed himself to be led, but he spared a moment to turn and glance over his shoulder. "Perhaps the major would like to accompany—"

"The major is wanted elsewhere," Lorna Maitland said, the coolness of her voice leaving Stephen in no doubt that he was *not* invited to join them. "He merely stopped a moment to give me his opinion on a matter, but now that he has done so, the subject is closed and he may go on about his business."

Having delivered her parting shot, she nudged the boy back up the gravel path. Within moments they had turned right and disappeared behind the tall, thick yews, presumably headed toward the bridge and the charming fish ponds that had replaced the moat, their ultimate destination the little rustic glade that shaded the stream.

Though Stephen could have shown them the way, he remained in the garden long after the sound of their footfalls had faded. He needed to think. He had made a fine mess of his first private encounter with Lorna Maitland—a fine mess, indeed, since seeing the young lady had been his only reason for accepting Paul Clement's invitation to accompany him to Clement Park.

Stephen could not return to Derbyshire to take care of important family matters, nor could he get on with his life; not until he had seen Lorna. His conscience would not let him.

The lady had corresponded with Paul in good faith, her first letters revealing her hesitancy about agreeing to a betrothal. With her later missives, however, all her doubts seemed to have faded, and she made him privy to her innermost thoughts and feelings.

Stephen had sensed the moment in which she had

fallen in love with Paul, and though he felt responsible for the situation, he had said nothing. How could he do so, when the letters had been his only shield against the horrors that surrounded him? God help him, he could not give them up!

To appease whatever principles he still possessed, Stephen had made a pact with himself, one that allowed him to continue with the deception. Should he and Paul both survive the war, he vowed to meet Miss Lorna Maitland. If, after seeing her with his own eyes, he believed she would be happy as the next Lady Clement, he would say nothing of the letters, merely bid her farewell and leave the engaged couple to formalize their nuptial arrangements.

Unfortunately, he had formulated no alternative plan should the couple clearly not suit.

Now, of course, Stephen knew he could not leave—not before he convinced Lorna that it would be a mistake for her to marry Paul Clement. The lady was pure sunshine, while Paul and his family were ice—frozen tundra that would soak up all the warmth she had to give, offering her none in return. They would never thaw, and she would be miserable in their company.

"Damnation!" he said, the angry utterance frightening the chiff chaff into abandoning its perch atop the rose trellis. "Why did I ever answer that first letter?"

Chapter Four

Lorna fell in love with the beautiful green glade, where a stand of tall beech trees formed a cathedrallike canopy above a noisy little stream—a stream whose cool clear water skipped over a pile of pale gray rocks. It was a thoroughly untamed spot, and she felt an immediate affinity with its simplicity and its naturalness.

When she first spied the collection of huge stones, Lorna fancied they had been tossed from on high, like pebbles from the hand of some mythical giant, and allowed to fall wherever they might. Dozens of the smaller stones formed an unintentional dam that held back a shallow pool—a pool where schools of little red-bellied minnows darted in and out of the shadows near the water's edge.

A fallen willow tree that had been overwhelmed by the dominant beeches formed a sort of footbridge across the water, giving access to a large, flat-topped boulder that was warmed by the sun. Naturally, such a Circe-like outcropping beckoned a lad of Thomas's age, and he willingly answered the summons. He made short work of scrambling across the trunk of the fallen willow and climbing to the top of the boulder, soon declaring to all within hearing of his voice that he was king of the world.

Thomas spent far too much time in the company of adults, and he was often serious beyond his years.

Rarely did Lorna see him behaving like a normal ten-year-old, and wishing to give him an opportunity to vent his youthful spirits, she had allowed him to strut and yell to his heart's content, never saying a word when he splashed water all down the front of his nankeens or muddied his boots and stockings while trying to capture an uncooperative tadpole. While the boy played, Lorna lifted the back of her skirt to protect the fabric, then disposed herself upon the mossy bank near the roots of the fallen willow. It was as good a place as any to calm her still-troubled senses.

How dare Major Rutledge presume to tell her that she should not marry Paul. By what right did he interfere in her life? Who gave him leave to judge how well she and Paul would suit?

After all, what was between a betrothed couple was private, and only that couple knew what had passed between them. Only they could know the sweet, tender words that had been spoken. Not, of course, that Paul had ever crossed the line in his correspondence. He had never spoken of love, only of his joy in her letters and of his unswerving friendship toward her. Still, his words had touched her heart, convincing her that he and she were perfectly suited to each other, regardless of the businesslike origins of their betrothal.

Granted, their first face-to-face meeting had been a disappointment. But what did that say to the matter? There was bound to be a little awkwardness when two people who had corresponded for the better part of a year, sharing their thoughts and dreams, finally looked into each other's eyes. Such an awkwardness was probably not unlike what a couple experienced the first time they shared a bed.

The instant that supremely intimate thought entered her head, Lorna was suffused with the heat of embarrassment—a heat so searing she feared she might faint. Not because she was nervous about what passed between a husband and wife in the privacy of their bedchamber, but because the man whose image had flashed before her eyes—his strong, naked arms gathering her close while his firm lips descending upon hers—was not Paul Clement!

The man she had pictured sharing her bed was neither slender nor divinely fair. To her chagrin, he was broad-shouldered and dark-haired, and he possessed teasing brown eyes.

Lorna refused to put a name to that man. In fact, she pushed the entire image from her mind, hoping she would forget it as though it had never happened. Fanning her heated face with her hands, she jumped to her feet and called to her cousin to come to her. "We must go, Thomas."

"Aw," he complained, "do we have to?"

"Now," she replied, her voice sterner than was her usual manner. "It will soon be time for dinner, and I must get dressed. I . . . I wish to look my best this evening, for my fiancé."

Lorna took an extra long time preparing herself for the evening, though whether it was to please her fiancé or to salve her conscience, she could not say. It was enough that the business of dressing with the dubious assistance of one of the parlor maids took her mind off all save her toilette.

In time, after her thick, straight hair had been thoroughly brushed through, then arranged in a loose knot atop her head, she allowed the young maid to assist her into a simply cut dinner dress of lilac sarcenet—a dress whose only embellishment was a row of small, dark purple beads that edged the short sleeves. In hopes of diverting attention from the gown's fashionably low-cut neckline, Lorna fastened around her throat a delicate silver necklace set with a pear-shaped amethyst.

She knew she need not be concerned that she would put Paul or his family to the blush, for though she lived in a small village, her clothes were made by one of London's premier modistes—her father insisted upon it. As well, her jewelry, though simple, was fashioned by the artisans at Rundel and Bridge. Though her taste was understated, she looked what she was—a young woman whose father could afford to purchase the best.

What she did not know, and Stephen Rutledge would have bet his life on the fact, was that she was absolutely beautiful. From the moment she entered the small yellow drawing room, where the family met before dinner, Stephen had been unable to take his eyes off her. The wool merchant's daughter was dressed simply but elegantly, and she carried herself with an air of serenity that would have put a princess to shame. He would have told her as much had she not given him the cut direct, choosing to seat herself on the opposite side of the room from him, and not once allowing him to claim her attention.

Dinner was a protracted, boring affair, served at a long mahogany table more suited to a party of forty than to the six people who took their places exactly at five of the clock. Paul, who had arrived just as the butler announced that the meal was served, had led his intended to the dining room, but once he had seated her, he went around to the other side of the ornately set table to sit beside Calvin Maitland.

Stephen was instructed to sit beside Miss Maitland, a situation he did not find in the least unpalatable. His dinner partner was of a different opinion, however, and only her sense of what was expected of a guest prompted her to reply to his rather innocuous remarks. Not that conversation was all that easy, for their chairs were positioned at least four feet apart. Still, the distance between the middle and the ends of the table made it impossible to speak to their host and hostess without shouting, and a pair of tall silver epergnes placed in the center of the table effectively obscured the lady's view of her fiancé and her father. For that reason, she had either to converse with Stephen or give her full attention to the food on her plate.

Taking advantage of the situation, Stephen leaned toward her slightly, speaking quietly, so only she could hear. "Is the roast duckling to your taste, Miss Maitland?"

She looked not at him but at the pattern of cutwork on the damask table cover. "Very nice," she replied, her tone unenthusiastic.

"And the asparagus? The sauce is quite good, would you not agree?"

Still looking at the cloth, she said, "Quite."

Not at all put off by her short replies, Stephen continued. "What condiment gives it that piquant taste? Do you know?"

"No."

Trying again, he phrased his question in a manner that would not prompt a monosyllabic answer. "What think you of this wine, Miss Maitland?"

As if to emphasize her displeasure at his conversational gambits, she lifted the water goblet to her lips and drank thirstily. After returning the crystal to the table, she said, "I do not care for wine."

"Ah," he said, as if she had given him something weighty to ponder. After a moment, he leaned toward her again, his voice quite low. "Forgive my persistence, madam, but what *do* you like?"

This time she looked at him. "Silent dinner partners," she replied.

Stephen was obliged to hide his laughter behind his

napkin, pretending a bout of coughing. Moments later, he sighed, then turned back to her, his voice filled with spurious resignation. "Oh, how sharper than a serpent's tooth to have a thankless dinner partner."

Her lips twitched ever so slightly, and though she subdued the smile that threatened to betray her, when she looked at him at last, she was unable to hide the amusement in her eyes. "Sir," she said, her toploftly tone not in the least convincing, "I consider it nothing less than sacrilege to misquote Shakespeare, and anyone who does so *deserves* to feel the sharpness of the serpent's tooth."

"Probably, madam, but who would catch the serpent so he might dispense the prescribed justice? You?"

When she could not suppress a shudder, Stephen chuckled. "If you do not care for serpents, may I suggest the substitution of a bee? I believe you are not uncomfortable handling those little creatures. Surely their 'sharp tooth' would serve as well."

"Oh, no," she said, "I could not do that."

"Never tell me, ma'am, that you have had a change of heart toward me."

"Not at all, Major. It is the bee whose well-being I would protect. Did you but know it, when the bee stings, he surrenders his stinger and his life as well. I would not punish an innocent creature."

"But you have no reservations about punishing a misquoter?"

She smiled sweetly, though there was a light of devilment in her eyes. "No, sir. No reservations whatsoever."

This time Stephen laughed aloud, and the sound gained the attention of the other four diners. The lady's father looked across the wide table, his expression clearly revealing his wish to take part in any conversation that would produce laughter, while the other three merely stared at the two offenders as if they had committed an unconscionable breach of etiquette.

"Miss Maitland," Lady Clement said, raising her voice so it carried down the long table to her guest, "when we leave the gentlemen to their port, please join me in my private apartment."

The recipient of this unlooked-for invitation stammered her acquiescence. "Th . . . thank you, ma'am. I should be pleased to join you."

If their hostess noticed the lack of eagerness in her guest's voice, she gave no indication. "It is time," she continued, "that we began filling out the cards of invitation to the party."

"Party?" Miss Maitland said. "Forgive me, ma'am, if I appear obtuse, but to what party do you refer?"

Lady Clement lifted an imperious brow, as though unaccustomed to being questioned. "The party to which I refer, Miss Maitland, is the one announcing your betrothal to my son. I wish to hold it on Friday. Any later, and the guests will have already read about it in the *Times*."

Stephen had never seen a prospective bride display less enthusiasm at the prospect of a coming betrothal party. Sitting next to her, he was privy to the lady's reaction—he would not call it enthusiasm—and it took the form of flared nostrils, clenched fists hidden in her lap, and a rapidly rising and falling bosom. Not that he had any complaint about the latter occurrence. With the combined aid of his added height and the fashionably low neckline of the lady's lilac sarcenet, he had a highly enjoyable view, and he was far more inclined to thank his hostess for inciting it.

Stephen glanced across the table to see if Paul had noticed his fiancée's tantalizing display of bosom, but the fellow was busy holding his wineglass up to the light cast by the ornate crystal chandelier, examining the clarity of the liquid. *Damnation!* Could the man not see what a beautiful woman Lorna Maitland was? Was he dead to all feeling?

Since honor decreed that Stephen limit to only a few seconds his perusal of the future bride's creamy orbs, he returned his attention to his former fellow officer. "Clement," he began, raising his voice so he might be heard, "I took a stroll in your garden this afternoon."

The lady in lilac gasped.

Ignoring the sound, Stephen continued. "The sun shone gloriously, making an hour out of doors quite enjoyable, and I could not help but wish you had been there, old boy. You might have pointed out to me one or two of the more interesting plants. Where were you, by the way?"

"Father and I rode to the village."

"Right," Sir Duncan added. "As you said, Major, the sun was shining and the weather was first-rate. No point in wasting a splendid afternoon by remaining indoors. After all, nothing important to keep us at home."

"No," Stephen replied, resisting the temptation to remind their host that he had a houseful of guests, "nothing at all."

For the next ten minutes there was only silence, and to Lorna's relief, Lady Clement finally placed her napkin beside her plate, indicating that the meal had come to an end and that the ladies should leave the gentlemen to their port. "I shall expect you in half an hour," she said once she and Lorna were outside the room. She did not add, "Do not keep me waiting," but there was no need, for her tone delivered the message all too clearly.

Not that Lorna wished to delay the meeting any longer than necessary, for there were a few matters that needed to be settled between her and her fiancé's parent. Lorna embraced the adage that it was better to begin as one meant to go on, and she had every intention of informing Lady Clement that *she*, and not her future mother-in-law, would say when it was time to send the betrothal announcement to the papers.

As it turned out, the after-dinner session with Lady Clement ended only moments after it began. Lorna had just been admitted to her ladyship's private apartment when the pickle-faced Simmons brought word that the cook had fallen and injured her knee.

"I must go belowstairs," Lady Clement said, "otherwise someone will take it upon themselves to send for the doctor. Servants always overdramatize these little mishaps."

If any accident can be called providential, Lorna supposed this one was it, for the cook's mishap prevented Lorna from saying something she might later regret. At that moment she was quite angry—with her ladyship and with a certain major who would not leave well enough alone—and anger was always a handicap when attempting to make one's sentiments known.

"Come to me tomorrow," Lady Clement said just before she followed the butler from the room. "At eleven. Do not be late, Miss Maitland."

Though she was more than happy to postpone this evening's meeting, the prospect of a morning tête-à-tête with her future mother-in-law did not fill Lorna with pleasure. And, if the truth be known, even had Lady Clement been the soul of diplomacy regarding the announcement, the idea of a betrothal party did not instill in Lorna the joy it should have done.

Before she could enter into any plans, she needed to speak with her fiancé. She would never had suspected that such a simple matter would prove so difficult, and when she went belowstairs only to find the four gentlemen already seated around a game table, engrossed in a rubber of whist that looked like it might last the entire evening, Lorna admitted defeat and returned to her room.

She tossed and turned all night. The combination of frustration and disappointment contrived to rob her of much needed sleep, and when morning came, she felt restless and totally out of sorts. Not wishing to encounter anyone until she had mastered her feelings, Lorna dressed without assistance, donning a green-sprigged muslin, then tossing a paisley shawl around her shoulders. Lastly, she removed her portable writing desk from the shelf of the chiffonnier.

After assuring herself that the slender wooden box was securely fastened, Lorna put it beneath her arm, then stole quietly down the servants' stairs and out the rear door. As she hurried around to the carriageway then over the limestone bridge, she spared only a moment to glance at the two fish ponds; they were lovely, but she sought the seclusion of the rustic glade she had discovered yesterday.

Once Lorna was beside the stream, seated on the mossy bank near the overturned willow tree, the soothing sound of the water flowing over the rocks worked its magic upon her troubled thoughts. In time, the tranquility of the place brought the peace that had eluded her last night.

She knew what she had to do. While a dignified little pied wagtail perched on the topmost of the boulders modulated his sharp *cheep, cheep* to something resembling a song, Lorna unlocked the slender writing desk, withdrew pen, inkpot, and paper and began a letter to Paul.

My dear friend,
    First, allow me to tell you how much your letters meant to me. Their warmth, their honesty instilled in

me a regard for you that I shall carry in my heart all the days of my life.

There is much I wish to say to you, and because we have always been able to speak freely on paper, I have chosen to express my thoughts in this manner. Permit me, if you will, to ask that question which is uppermost in my mind. It is imperative that I know your answer. Do you wish to make public the under-standing between us? Are you still

Lorna paused, then she quickly scratched through the last two lines. If she must ask a question, let it be the one whose answer she truly wished to know. Though seared by the heat of embarrassment at the very thought of so forward a query, she dipped her stylus into the rose-painted inkpot and wrote: *Do you truly wish to marry me?*

There! She had said it. Now, if Paul would reply with the same forthrightness, she would know where she stood.

At some time during the previous night, Lorna had come to a decision. She had resolved to live out the possible three-score-and-ten years of her life as a lonely old maid, rather than spend even one day as the wife of an unwilling husband.

Realizing what she must do, she had resolutely placed the ribbon-tied stack of Paul's letters, along with the miniature, in the drawer of her bed table. "It is best," she had whispered to the little table, as though it knew what she had done, "if I am not influenced by the lovely words Paul wrote me during the past eleven months, or by the memory of how I fell in love with his handsome face."

The letters, as dear as they were to Lorna, needed to be relegated to the past. Now, today, she must deal with the man who wrote them. She must know if she and Paul Clement had a future together.

Before she had an opportunity to complete the letter she had begun, Lorna heard footfalls on the narrow, leaf-strewn path leading to the glade. Perhaps it was her embarrassment at the forwardness of the missive that caused her to panic, or maybe it was simply her wish to keep anyone from asking questions; whatever the reason, she shoved the inkpot and pen back into the portable writing desk, then hurriedly closed the lid. Only after she had pressed the metal lock did she realize her letter to Paul had fallen to the ground.

With the intruder mere seconds away, Lorna looked around her for a place to hide the uncompleted letter, and spying a hole in the overturned willow, she quickly wadded the sheet of paper into a ball, then stuffed it into that hole. She had only just straightened, folding her hands in her lap as though she had been employed in nothing more serious than a contemplation of the red-bellied minnows in the shallow pool, when Major Rutledge approached her.

Dressed in York tan breeches that hugged his muscular thighs and a sable-colored jacket that was only slightly darker than his hair, he looked quite handsome. Not as handsome as Paul, of course, but honesty compelled Lorna to admit that any woman would find the major's dark eyes and that ready smile—

Surprised at where her undisciplined thoughts were headed, she forced them from her mind. Of what possible interest could it be to her if women found Stephen Rutledge appealing? True, he had a way of looking deeply into a person's eyes, as if he was interested in who she was and what she had to say, but the impression was probably a trick of the light. After all, why should he be looking at her in that manner? It was *Paul* who should have been—

No! She refused as well to let her thoughts go there. Paul was Paul, and Stephen Rutledge was a different person entirely.

"Good morning, Miss Maitland," he said, inclining his head in an abbreviated bow. " 'Tis a lovely day, is it not?"

He did not seem in the least surprised to see her, and for an instant it crossed Lorna's mind that he might have followed her to the glade. Pure fancy, of course, for why would he seek her out when they were virtual strangers? As if privy to her thoughts, he said, "One wonders, madam, if you are following me. First the garden, and now this verdant retreat."

"*I* following *you*? Sir, I—"

"It happens all the time," he said, sighing as if required to support a heavy burden. "Young ladies take one look at me, and the next thing I know, I am being obliged to beat them off with a stick."

At the thought of this large, muscular man needing to take up arms to defend himself against a female, Lorna felt a smile quivering upon her lips. Though she tried to suppress that smile, she found she could not do so. "Major, are you never serious?"

"Oh, but I am quite serious. As it happens, I came to the glade for no other purpose than to seek just such a stick. Not too big a weapon, mind you—I should dislike doing actual injury to a member of the weaker sex—but one adequate for the job."

"One wonders," Lorna said, "since Lady Clement and I are the only females in residence, which of us you suppose will pursue you with such zealousness that you must defend yourself?"

He sighed again. "Who can say, Miss Maitland? Who can say?"

"Who, indeed."

Without waiting for an invitation, he lowered himself onto the ground quite close to Lorna—so close she detected a hint of his sandalwood shaving soap . . . so close his shoulder brushed against hers— and the brief contact brought, unbidden, the realization that such a muscular man must also be quite powerful. She had no doubt that Stephen Rutledge could sweep a woman into his arms with little or no effort and carry her wherever he, and the woman, wished to go.

When Lorna let herself wonder how it would feel to be swept up into those strong arms, her obliging imagination supplied the answer, and to her chagrin the image caused several unlooked-for and very disquieting sensations inside her.

She chose not to ponder the reason why her breath had caught in her throat, or why her stomach felt as if a pair of hummingbirds had been trapped inside her and were furiously fluttering their wings in hopes of getting out. Instead, to dispel those sensations, she concentrated on the man's intrusion upon her privacy. "If, as you say, Major, you came in search of a stick, I fear you will find nothing suitable here. Perhaps you should explore the bank on the far side of the stream."

She pointed toward the stretch of stones Thomas had used yesterday to reach the largest of the boulders. "Just keep to the rocks, sir, and you will have no trouble getting to the other side."

He glanced in the direction of her pointing finger, but he made no effort to follow her advice. Instead, he settled in comfortably, with one long leg stretched out in front of him and the other bent so the knee was raised, allowing him to prop his right arm upon it. With his arm propped, his hand was in the direct line of Lorna's vision, and she could not avoid noticing his long, tapered fingers, or the thick, powerful-looking wrist that showed beneath the sleeve of his coat. If the truth be told, she had difficulty forcing her attention elsewhere.

Though annoyed with herself for acting like a silly schoolroom chit, she was even more exasperated with *him* for being obtuse regarding her hints that he should leave. "Sir," she said rather sharply, "I was writing a letter."

"Pray, do not let me impede your progress, ma'am. Write as much as you wish. I assure you, the scratching of the pen will not disturb me."

Sorely tested, Lorna said, "For this letter, Major Rutledge, I need solitude."

The smile he gave her was as fatuous as it was spurious. "I shall be as quiet as a mouse."

The man was impossible! Subtle hints directed at him clearly fell short of their mark. Lorna had begun to think she might have to find a stick for her own purposes when she noticed a honeybee hovering just above his hand. "Do not move," she said, the tone of her voice low and quite serious.

Stephen obeyed instantly, all teasing put aside. Not so very many weeks had passed since he was in the thick of battle, and his reflexes were still finely honed to react to possible danger. When someone warned him not to move, he listened.

"A bee has been attracted to the scent of your shaving soap," Miss Maitland said, "but if you will remain still, so that he knows you pose no threat to him, I am persuaded he will fly away."

The lady had only just finished assuring him that he was in no immediate danger, when the bee lit on the back of Stephen's wrist, just below his coat sleeve. Lulled by her assurances, Stephen was startled when he felt a sudden white-hot stinging. "Damnation!" he muttered, slapping instinctively at the little insect with the powerful bite.

The instant the innocent-looking culprit fell to the

ground, unmoving, Miss Maitland rose to her knees and caught hold of Stephen's wrist. "Here," she said, her tone brooking no argument, "let me extract the stinger. You will feel much better once the source of the poison is gone."

While she spoke, she pinched his skin between her thumb and finger, and using her fingernail, she gently flicked out the tiny briarlike stinger. "Have you any tobacco, sir?"

Startled by the seeming non sequitur, Stephen said, "Not with me. Were you desirous of blowing a cloud, Miss Maitland?"

She looked up at him then, and for just a moment a smile played upon her lips. "A bit of dampened tobacco placed upon the point of entry would draw out the venom."

With the removal of the stinger, Stephen had felt better, and the burning in his skin was fading by the moment. "I am fine," he assured her. "You need have no concern for me."

She shook her head. "Larger men than you have been felled by a little honeybee. Some people are more susceptible than others to the venom. Here," she said, "allow me to feel your pulse to see if it has accelerated."

Assuming she meant to check the pulse in his wrist, Stephen turned his hand over. To his surprise, she ignored the proffered pulse point; instead, she reached up and slipped her fingers inside the collar of his shirt. With an air of one who knows what she is doing, she pressed her fingertips against the side of his neck, then placed her other hand inside his coat and flattened her palm against his chest. "Those who react to the sting," she said, "experience a shortness of breath as well as a quickened heart rate. How is your breathing?"

Labored, Stephen thought, most definitely labored,

and his heart had picked up its pace as well. It was
not the bee sting his body was reacting to, however;
it was the pleasurable sensation caused by Lorna
Maitland's warm hands sliding inside his clothing.

"Forgive me," she said, "if I muss your neckcloth."

"Think nothing of it," he replied, all the while
knowing that *he* could think of nothing else but the
feel of her hand pressed against his skin.

*Steady, old boy! Inhale deeply. Give yourself a moment
or two to catch your breath, and do not allow your
thoughts to dwell upon the hour or so you would like to
spend enjoying Lorna Maitland's caresses.* It was good
advice. Unfortunately, his body paid no heed to the
counsel.

Stephen could think of nothing but his desire to
touch Lorna as she was touching him. He longed to
slide his hand along the side of her slender neck, feel
her satiny skin against his palm, then continue
around to her lovely nape so he might urge her face
close to his. Urge her mouth toward—

What was happening here? Stephen had meant only
to assure himself that the lady truly wished to wed
Paul Clement. Now here he was imagining himself
pulling her against his chest and kissing her until she
forgot everything but him—until she forgot that Paul
Clement had ever existed.

While the object of his fantasy continued to moni-
tor his pulse, Stephen searched her face for a sign
that she might be aware of the unexpected direction
his errant thoughts had taken. Apparently her
thoughts had not run parallel to his, and if she was
concerned with anything not related to bee stings,
she gave no indication. Granted, there was a slight
rosy glow to her lovely cheeks, but in all other ways
the lady appeared perfectly normal . . . and so calm
she might have been ministering to her young cousin.

Chapter Five

*P*retend *he is your Cousin Thomas!* Lorna kept repeating that phrase to herself. Or imagine he is a stray dog. Or better yet, a fence post. Anything but this large, incredibly masculine man whose very life force beat like a drum against her fingertips.

When she had reached up to touch Stephen Rutledge, her motives had been completely without guile. She had wanted only to assure herself that he was not reacting adversely to the bee venom. As it turned out, *he* appeared to be fine. It was *she* who was reacting as though some foreign substance had invaded her bloodstream, making her feel dizzy and warm all over.

She was acting as though she had never touched a man before. Actually, she had never done so—not as intimately as she was touching Stephen Rutledge—but that was no excuse for letting her emotions run away with her. No reason to fantasize about allowing her fingers to touch more than his strong neck. No reason to grow weak in the knees from imagining how it would feel to slide her hands inside his shirt and smooth her palms across his broad shoulders.

To Lorna's relief, she was saved from committing such an unseemly act by the sound of footfalls on the leaf-strewn path that lead to the glade. Unfortunately, her relief was short-lived, for the newest visitor was none other than her fiancé. And if the surprised—nay, shocked—look on his face was anything to judge by, he completely misinterpreted what he saw.

"I beg your pardon," Paul Clement said, his tone icily formal. "I had no idea anyone was here."

Lorna wanted to scream in frustration. She had done everything she could think of to find some time alone with her betrothed, and now he had come upon her at the one moment she wished he had not. She must appear quite wanton, kneeling before Stephen Rutledge, her hands inside his clothing. As for those fantasies of more intimate explorations, Lorna offered up her thanks to the powers that be that neither gentleman could see inside her head.

"Paul," she said, hastily shoving her hands behind her back, as if they had committed some act for which they must be banished, "allow me to explain." When embarrassment caused her brain to go blank, Lorna looked imploringly at the major, hoping one man could find a way to explain to another man what must appear a rather compromising situation.

"Felled by a bee," the major said, not in the least disconcerted. "Miss Maitland was merely ascertaining the degree of damage. To my everlasting gratitude, the sting was not mortal. Venial, perhaps, but not mortal."

If her fiancé found the pun amusing, he kept the fact well hidden. Though the expression on his finely chiseled face was as animated as Lorna had ever seen it, she suspected his anger had more to do with affronted pride than with jealousy, and her suspicions were proven correct when he gave her his opinion of behavior unbecoming a lady.

"A lady," he said, "especially one who aspires to a title of some importance, should conduct herself in such a manner that her actions are never subject to question and, therefore, need no explanation."

The major made a *tsk-tsk* noise that infuriated Lorna and did nothing to placate her fiancé. "But, Clement, old fellow, what would you have had the lady do? Should she have stood by, wringing her hands, while I fell victim to a possible seizure?"

Paul pinned the larger man with a cold stare. "A lady would not have been here unchaperoned. Ergo, she might have wrung her hands as much as she liked, for her services would not have been needed."

Having delivered his opinion, Paul Clement bowed stiffly, then turned and walked away.

"Wait!" Lorna called.

As ill luck would have it, when she attempted to rise, her shawl became entangled with her feet, and she would have pitched forward onto the mossy ground if Stephen had not caught her by the arms and supported her until she regained her balance.

"Steady," he said.

Instead of thanking him for saving her from a nasty fall, Lorna railed at him for his flippant attitude. "Why must you always provoke Paul into saying things that show him in a bad light? One might almost think you do it on purpose."

"Acquit me, madam."

She attempted to pull free of his supporting hands, but the major tightened his grip, obliging her to remain. When she looked up at him, his expression was as serious as she had ever seen it. "You are an intelligent woman, Lorna, so think on this: Though I might have provoked Paul into saying more than he meant to say, I have not the power to make him give voice to something he does not believe."

He released her then, and Lorna took a step back, putting some distance between them. She did not wish to confront the logic of his observation about

Paul. At that moment, she did not even want to consider the implications, and for that reason she concentrated instead on the one part of the major's remark that would allow her to avoid all the rest. "Who gave you leave to use my name? I never did so, and no gentleman would take such a liberty without—"

"Lorna, Lorna, Lorna." All seriousness had left his face and a wicked gleam sparkled in his eyes. "If we must speak of taking liberties, allow me to remind you that it was *you* who put your hand inside my coat. It was that very liberty that made me think you meant our relationship to be on a more intimate footing."

"You thought no such thing!"

He made a great show of straightening his neckcloth and waistcoat, as though she had left him disheveled. "It quite shocked me, actually. Here was I, practically at death's door, alone and defenseless, and you took advantage of my weakness by making free with my person."

"Of all the whiskers! That is not the way it happened, and you know it."

He shrugged his broad shoulders. "All I know, madam, is that I feared for my honor. And me without that stick I had come to the glade to find. Did I not tell you I would need one?"

Lorna was obliged to smother a chuckle, and not willing to let him see that his foolishness had amused her, she pulled her shawl more securely around her shoulders, then bent to retrieve the portable writing desk. Once the slender box was tucked beneath her arm, she turned toward the footpath. "Your elaborate reshaping of the truth convinces me that you have suffered no ill effects from the bee sting. Therefore, I shall leave you, Major Rutledge, and go in search of my fiancé."

She hurried off, and Stephen let her go. When the sound of her soft footfalls faded into the distance, he walked over to the willow tree, where he had seen Lorna sitting earlier, then bent forward and removed the crumpled paper she had stuffed into the hole.

Lorna spied Paul just ahead of her on the carriage-way. Though he was quite near the wide covered portico at the front of the house, and she had only just crossed the limestone bridge between the two fish ponds, she was within calling distance. Happy to have found him so easily, she had drawn breath to call to him when she heard the jingling of harness and the slow rumble of wheels upon the carriageway behind her.

"Deuce take it!" she muttered inelegantly, "what now?"

Turning, Lorna spied a dilapidated cane gig pulled by an aging, dappled-gray horse, the type that could be hired at most any posting inn. The youth handling the ribbons wore a cap and workman's smock, while the dark-haired vision sitting beside him wore a wide-poked silk bonnet trimmed in delicate grebe feathers, a fashionable poplin traveling dress, and a three-quarter pelisse of willow green—a shade of green, Lorna knew from experience, that would match to perfection the wearer's eyes.

The newcomer waved her parasol above her head in excited greeting. "Lorna," she called. "Wait! It is I, Analise."

Lorna waited. She could not do otherwise. After all, the beautiful flibbertigibbet coming toward her was a member of her family, if only by marriage. Yet while she molded her lips into something resembling a smile, Lorna balled her hands into fists to help ease her frustration at having been thwarted once again in her attempt to find a moment alone with her fiancé.

Blast the woman! Having absented herself for nearly a month without so much as a word of explanation or a note to her son, why must Analise Whidby show up now? And why here, where she was least wanted?

The driver reined in the aging horse and held the animal steady while his passenger stepped down from the gig. When she had reached the ground safely, she turned and smiled at the young ostler, a gesture that inspired in the youth a look of slavish devotion. "You were most kind," she said. "I do not know what I would have done if you had not brought me here. I shall not soon forget you, my hero of the road."

Though Lorna blushed at such theatrics, it was a fact that Analise depended upon males—no matter their age and social standing—to assist her over life's little rough spots. And though she failed to offer the driver the customary gratuity, he seemed satisfied with her smile. "Drive on around to the stable," she directed. "I am persuaded someone there will know what to do with my things."

After touching his cap respectfully, the youth did as he was instructed and continued around to the rear of the house to deliver the trunk and portmanteau that were strapped to the back of the vehicle.

"My dear," Analise said, pressing her still youthful cheek against Lorna's, "how are you?" Not waiting for an answer, she said, "I vow it took me forever to get here, and I am in desperate need of a cup of tea."

Completely disregarding the fact that she had shown up at an estate where she was unknown and uninvited, the lady slipped her arm through Lorna's and began to stroll toward the pink marblestone facade. "What a handsome house. Who do we know here?"

Lorna gasped. Analise was nearing thirty, but she

was still as scatterbrained as a schoolgirl, and as bird-witted as she was beautiful, but this latest disregard of the conventions was foolish even for her. Exasperated, Lorna said, "Where have you been? And why have you come here?"

At the sharply voiced questions, the young widow's coal black brows lifted in astonishment. Choosing to misunderstand the first question, she said, "I have been at Epping Grange, where I was treated with a warmer welcome than you have shown me. Pilcher told me that you, my son, and Calvin were here, and that is why I have come. "

"You should not have done so."

Analise blinked, allowing her long, sooty eyelashes to linger for just a moment against her satiny skin—a tactic that usually got her whatever she wanted from any male between the ages of six and sixty. Understandably, with Lorna that particular little trick fell short of its mark.

"It may interest you to know, Analise, that Sir Duncan and Lady Clement were barely tolerant of Thomas's arrival, and they insist that he remain abovestairs in the nursery. What they will say when another of my relatives is foisted upon them, I cannot say."

"Oh, pooh." The widow waved her gloved hand toward the large, turreted manor house. "In a residence that size, what can one more guest matter?"

"If the guest is uninvited, she can set the entire household at sixes and sevens."

Lorna cut short her reproach; what was the use? Like oil and water, logic and Analise Whidby did not mix. Furthermore, Lorna was not nearly as interested in her shatterbrained relative's comings and goings as she was in the rather odd behavior of her fiancé, who was walking toward them at a decidedly brisk pace.

When the gig first arrived, she noticed that Paul had remained beside one of the columns of the portico, presumably waiting to see what visitor had come to Clement Park. Upon spying the newcomer, however, he surprised Lorna by reacting in a most unexpected manner, first gripping the column as if needing its support, then releasing it and hurrying down the carriageway toward the two women.

Even at a distance, Lorna could see that his face was more animated than it had been at any other time since her arrival. The wind had tousled his blond hair, making him appear relaxed and almost boyish, and in his gray eyes was a look of wonder, as if he had just been granted his most cherished wish. Here was the welcome Lorna had hoped for—hoped for but never received—and her fiancé was lavishing it all upon a stranger.

When he was still several feet away, Paul paused, his gaze riveted on Analise. The diminutive lady was at that moment supplying Lorna with a disjointed explanation for her disappearance from Tunbridge Wells, and because she was obliged to look up at her much taller relative, the wide poke of her bonnet concealed most of her face from the gentleman.

Paul seemed not to notice, and while Lorna watched in mortified fascination, he gave himself the pleasure of looking Analise over from her feather-trimmed bonnet to her kid traveling boots, his appraisal almost worshipful as it measured every inch of her trim figure. When he could contain his joy no longer, he extended his hands in warmest greeting.

"Beatrice," he said, the word a blend of reverence and raw hunger, "you have returned."

Chapter Six

"Beatrice," Paul said again, "I cannot believe you are here at last."

Analise turned to look at the man whose hands were stretched toward her in greeting. "Good day," she said. "Were you speaking to me?"

Lorna heard a ringing in her ears, a sort of death knell. It tolled once when she watched the joy on Paul's face when he thought Analise was this Beatrice person; it tolled a second time when she saw the despair that filled his eyes when he discovered his mistake. Lorna had wanted to know if Paul returned her affection, and now she had her answer. She knew in that instant that Paul would never love her as she wished to be loved.

Whoever Beatrice was, and wherever she was at that moment, she carried with her every ounce of Paul Clement's affection.

Though practically reeling from this revelation, Lorna managed somehow to speak, even to smile, and to pretend that she had not just received a blow to her heart and to her self-esteem. "Analise," she said, "allow me to present Lieutenant Paul Clement." Lorna's voice seemed to echo in her ears, as though she stood in some cavernous enclosure—a cold, unwelcoming enclosure. "Paul, this is Analise Whidby."

Analise was far from needle-witted, but her *ton* was good, and if she realized the gentleman had mis-

taken her for someone else—someone important—
she had enough social acumen to keep the knowledge to herself. The dark haired beauty offered Paul
her hand. "How do you do, Lieutenant?"

A strained look came over Paul's handsome face,
as though someone had stolen something valuable
from him, leaving him with no choice but to be brave
about the loss, but he recovered enough to take the
newcomer's proffered hand and bow over it. Following the dictates of proper behavior, he lifted her
gloved fingers to within an inch of his lips, then
straightened and released her. "Miss Whidby," he
said.

"Actually," Analise replied, "it is Mrs." She lowered her long lashes for a moment, then after a dramatic pause, she looked up into Paul's eyes. "I am
a widow."

For once, that tactic appeared to fail with a member of the opposite sex, and Lorna hurried to add,
"She is young Thomas's mother,"

Paul stared at his intended as if only just realizing
she was there. "Thomas? I do not believe I know
anyone by that—"

"My cousin. Thomas Whidby."

When Paul continued to stare blankly at her, she
added, "The lad in the nursery."

"Ah, yes." Returning his attention to Analise, Paul
asked, "Are you come for your son, ma'am? I cannot
think he would find much to entertain him here."

"Pshaw," replied the doting parent, "children are
such resilient creatures. They always find something
to keep them occupied. Besides, I would not *think* of
taking Lorna and her father away when they have
only just arrived. I shall just wait here quietly until
they are ready to return to Epping Grange. With your
permission, of course, Lieutenant."

"Of course," Paul replied. "I will instruct Simmons to see that a room is prepared."

If his response was less than enthusiastic, the beauty chose to ignore the fact. What Lorna could not ignore was the audible sigh Analise had breathed after having skillfully skirted the suggestion that she take her child and leave.

It was Lorna's turn to sigh, for unless she missed her guess, Analise Whidby was in trouble again, and the sooner Lorna took her hapless relative to Calvin Maitland, the sooner he could set things right. With that objective in mind, she put her own concerns aside for the moment, linked her arm through Analise's, and began walking toward the portico. "Come," she said, "let us find my father."

"Yes," Analise agreed quickly, "let us find Calvin, for I . . . I need to speak with him."

Civility required that Paul accompany them, and though he matched his pace with theirs, it was obvious his thoughts were elsewhere. He stared straight ahead, never once looking at either woman, and Lorna suspected that he did not hear a word of Analise's nonstop chatter about the latest *on dits* from Tunbridge Wells. Not that *she* heard more than a word here and there, just enough to allow her to mutter monosyllabic responses at what seemed appropriate intervals. Still, she was happy to let the other woman talk.

After the soul-shattering revelations concerning her fiancé's affections, Lorna did not think she could have spoken to Paul if her life depended upon it. She had been trying to talk with him for two days, but now she needed time in which to think—time to digest the knowledge that he loved another, time to decide how this new knowledge would change the understanding between them.

When they reached the house, Paul asked a footman if he knew where Mr. Maitland might be found.

"I believe he is in the billiard room, sir, with the young gentleman. Shall I inform him that you wish to see him?"

Paul shook his head. "Show Miss Maitland to her father, then take a message to the housekeeper that we have another guest."

His instructions given, Paul excused himself on the pretext of informing his mother of Mrs. Whidby's arrival. With a quick bow in their general direction, he left them to the footman and hurried up the stairs to the next level, his boots echoing loudly as he made his way down the corridor toward the door to the blue drawing room.

"Mama!"

The instant the two ladies were ushered into the masculine, teak-paneled room, young Thomas threw down his billiard cue, rushed across the bright turkey carpet, and threw his arms around his mother's slender, green-clad waist.

"Mama," he cried again, "you have returned at last!"

Those words were so like what Paul had uttered earlier, that Lorna felt wounded anew. Why did Paul not tell her that he loved another? Why lead her to believe that he was heart free, when all the time someone named Beatrice filled his thoughts? *Why? Why? Why?*

She knew what her father would answer to that question. She could almost hear his words. "These days," he would say, "money speaks with a powerful voice."

Though Lorna had thought better of Paul, she could only assume that when the "powerful voice" had spoken, Paul Clement had listened. Not that she blamed him overmuch for wishing to make an advantageous marriage; after all, such alliances were formed all the time. A son or daughter from a prestigious family might even be *expected* to marry someone who brought wealth to the union.

Still, Lorna could wish Paul had been honest about his feelings. He need not have written her such beautiful letters—letters that made her believe theirs would be a union of friends . . . of lovers.

Had he been honest, she might have agreed to an engagement on the strength of her own attraction to him. Many marriages began with less. Now, of course, she felt betrayed, and under the circumstances, she was not altogether certain she could continue with the betrothal.

"I knew it!" Calvin Maitland said, his tone all but yanking Lorna from her reverie. "Curse the fellow. I knew something was not right."

Thinking her father had somehow become privy to her discovery of Paul's true feelings, Lorna's face grew warm with embarrassment. When she looked at Calvin Maitland, however, she was grateful to see that his comments had been meant for another. He stood on the far side of the room, and he was staring directly at Analise, who sat in one of the red, leather-covered wing chairs that flanked the fireplace. She was dabbing her damp eyes with a sodden wisp of linen and lace.

"But, Calvin," she said between bouts of tears, "how was I to know Mr. Treherne would turn ugly?"

"How were you to know!"

Her questioner shoved his hands behind his back and locked his fingers together securely, as if afraid he might throttle the simpleton if he were not restrained. "Analise Whidby, if you possessed only half your looks and twice your brains, you'd still be a beautiful idgit!"

The object of his wrath blinked watery green eyes. "You think me beautiful, Calvin? Truly? I often wondered, but you never said so before."

Not surprisingly, Calvin Maitland's face turned a dangerous shade of purple, prompting Lorna to rush around the billiard table to stand beside him should he need restraining. "Papa," she said quietly, "calm yourself. You know there is nothing to be gained from scolding Analise, for she hears only what she wishes to hear."

"But to take money from a stranger! Whatever could have possessed her? She might have known he would want something in return."

"But he seemed so kind," Analise replied. "And though he was not as refined as most of the other gentlemen one meets in Tunbridge Wells, everyone said he had pots and pots of money. 'Rich as creases,' everyone said."

"Croesus!" Calvin roared.

Analise resorted to her handkerchief again. "I know I acted foolishly, but you do not need to curse at me."

While Lorna explained who Croesus was, her father strode angrily around the room, muttering beneath his breath with each step. Only when he chanced upon Thomas, who stood at the window embrasure, a pinched look upon his freckled face, did he cease his ranting. "Thee's got no call to worry, lad," he said, placing his hand upon the boy's shoulder. "I may wish to murder thy mother, but thee knows I'd not harm a hair on her head."

"I . . . I know, sir. It is just—"

"It is just that she's your mother, and you wish to protect her from growling old bears like me. The sentiment does you proud, lad, and I'd not have you behave any other way."

Thomas managed to smile. "You are not so very old, are you, sir?"

"Old enough to know better than to pursue a young widow only a few years older than my daughter. Which is more than I can say for that loose screw Felix Treherne." Recalled to Analise's latest scrape, he returned his attention to her. "How old is the fellow?"

Analise had the grace to blush. "Not much above fifty."

"Fifty! Fiend seize it, woman! Why do you not try your luck with a young man?"

"Because I *like* older men. They know about things like talking to lawyers and hiring butlers. Besides, all the young men want is . . ." She hesitated, glanced toward her son, then blushed again. "You know what the young men want of a widow."

"And you think Treherne wanted anything different?"

With this, Analise sat up straight, her pretty chin jutting stubbornly. "Felix wanted to marry me!"

"Then why in blazes did you flee from him?"

"I . . . I did not wish to marry him. I do not wish to marry again. And when I told him so, in the very kindest possible way, I assure you, he showed his true colors."

"Came the ugly did he?"

"Quite. He insisted that I repay the full sum he had paid the grocer and all those other bothersome tradesmen who had begun accosting me in the street, insisting that I settle their bills."

She looked toward Lorna, appealing to her for understanding. "Men can be so unreasonable at times. Is it not logical that if I could not pay the tradesmen, I could not repay Felix? He must have known that if I had possessed any money of my own, I never would have allowed him to settle the bills."

Lorna cleared her throat, as if stalling for time while she chose her words. "I will agree that Mr. Treherne sounds a most unreasonable fellow, and I hope you will forgive me if I appear similarly intractable. However, there is something I must know. Just how much had he expended on your behalf?"

Analise waved her hand in a negligent manner. "You know I have no head for figures."

"How much?" Lorna repeated.

"A few hundred. Perhaps a bit more."

"Analise," Calvin said, a warning tone to his voice, "spare us your evasions. Let us have a true accounting without further roundaboutation."

The beauty sighed, as if much put upon. "If you must know, it was somewhere in the neighborhood of two thousand guineas."

"Two thousand! Damnation, woman, that is a very expensive neighborhood. No wonder the man wanted his pound of flesh. I suppose when you refused his offer of marriage, he expected you to discharge the debt by becoming his mist—"

"Papa! Remember, little pitchers have big ears."

At his daughter's reminder, Calvin Maitland glanced toward the window embrasure. "Your pardon, lad. I quite forgot you were there."

His attention recalled by a new bout of sobs from the boy's mother, Calvin removed a fresh handkerchief from inside his coat, strode over to the red leather wing chair, and tossed the linen into Analise's lap. "Wipe your tears, there's a good girl, and tell us the whole story."

Though Analise dried her tearstained face, her words were punctuated by an occasional sniffle. "You . . . you cannot know how frightened I was," she began. "I explained to Felix that under no circumstances would I become his . . er . . . that is to say, I refused his alternative offer. Still, he would not leave me alone. He hounded me. Wherever I went, there he was. The opera, a private party, no matter how discreetly I slipped away from my lodgings, Felix always seemed to know which invitations I had accepted, and he would be there before me.

"Finally, when my nerves failed me, I stopped going out altogether. Even that did not serve. If I remained indoors, Felix, or one of his minions, was always to be found by the lamppost across the street from my lodgings. That is why I sent Thomas to you at Epping Grange, so he need not become a prisoner in his own home."

"You should have come with him," Calvin remarked. "Why did you not do so?"

When Analise merely shrugged her pretty shoulders, Lorna asked her own question. "What I do not understand is why, if you were without sufficient funds, you did not apply to Father? You know he never refuses you."

"That is just it," she said, a new supply of tears spilling down her cheeks. "He is always so good." She looked toward her benefactor, her damp eyes for once free of coquetry. "Calvin has been more than generous to me, and I . . . I could not tell him I had outrun my allowance again."

"Why ever not?" Calvin asked.

"Because I knew you would rail at me."

"Heaven preserve me, woman!"

"See. I told you he would rail at me."

"Of all the hen-witted women it has ever been my misfortune to—" He drew a deep breath, then let it out slowly. "Am I such an ogre that you preferred to put yourself under obligation to some reprobate who—"

"Papa! Little pitchers!"

By sheer strength of will, Calvin Maitland managed to swallow his anger. "Sorry," he mumbled. "Forgot again."

As apologies go, it lacked finesse, but the matter became moot immediately, for someone scratched at the billiard room door.

"Enter," Lorna called.

Simmons, the very proper butler, stepped just inside the room and bowed stiffly. "Her ladyship has ordered a nuncheon to be served in the breakfast parlor within the half hour."

Though his manner implied that he felt himself too superior a servant to be obliged to carry messages to lesser beings, Lorna thanked him as though he had shown every courtesy. "Inform Lady Clement that we will join her directly."

Lorna was relieved that they were to dine in the small, less formal breakfast parlor, for her nerves were stretched to the limit, and she did not think she could endure another silent meal eaten in the stuffy, oversized dining room, the only sound that of silver clinking against the china plates. It quite chilled her bones to think of spending an hour or more staring at her host and hostess seated at the far ends of the long mahogany table, and her fiancé seated across from her, the distance between them prohibiting any sort of conversation.

As it turned out, she need not have been concerned about the possible formality of the meal, for their hostess did not join them in the pale cream and maroon parlor. Sir Duncan and Paul were absent as well, and when Lorna's father spied the three places set at the oval-shaped parlor table and discovered that he and his ladies were to eat alone, he turned on the hapless footman who had been delegated to serve them in lieu of the butler. "Where the deuce have our host and hostess got to?"

"Sir, I . . . I—"

"And now I think of it, where is that whey-faced butler? Never tell me he thinks himself too good to wait upon us."

The embarrassed footman stammered an apology. "Your pardon, sir, but Mr. Simmons is . . . what I mean to say is . . . he said I was to . . ."

"Out with it man!"

His chin quivering, the footman informed them that the butler was serving the family, who were partaking of their nuncheon in the blue withdrawing room.

"The devil, you say!"

Though no one was more affronted than Lorna at this obvious snub, she tried to soothe her father's ruffled feathers. "The family probably wanted to give us an opportunity to visit privately with Analise."

Lorna wished she could believe her own words, but she could not. If the new arrival had her doubts about the situation, for once that matron had the sense to keep her thoughts to herself. As for Calvin Maitland, he said nothing more; he merely stared fixedly at the white damask cloth on the table. He had stopped blustering and turned quiet. It was a bad sign—a fact to which anyone who had done business with the wool merchant could have attested.

"Is this my fault?" Analise asked hesitantly. When no one answered her question, she said, "Perhaps I should not have shown up at a gentleman's residence uninvited." At the continued silence, her eyes filled with tears. "I should not have come."

"As ter that, lass, I'm thinking we should none of us have come."

Calvin had reached over and patted Analise's hand, and though his comment was directed at her, he looked at his daughter, watching for her reaction. " 'Tis a cold, drafty house, this ancient pile of stones, and I begin to long for the comforts of Epping Grange."

After a rather long pause, he said, "What say you, Lorna, my girl? Do you miss the warmth of home?"

The double meaning in the question did not escape Lorna. However, she was too confused at the moment to address either issue. Like her father, she was angered by the cold disregard for their feelings shown by Paul's parents, but she was also hurt and disillusioned by what she had learned of the man himself. "We cannot leave after only two days, Papa."

"We can," he replied quietly, "if that is your wish."

"It is not that simple."

"Then we'll make it simple."

She shook her head. "I understand your desire to be gone from the place, but we were invited for a fortnight. Let us remain at least through the weekend."

"You are sure that is what you wish to do, lass?"

She nodded. "I must, Papa. I have not yet had sufficient time alone with my fiancé, and I am persuaded that he and I must—"

"Fiancé!" Analise's mouth fell open. "Are you and the lieutenant engaged?"

"Nothing's official," Calvin said. "Our coming here was but a meeting to explore the possibilities. And I, for one, have seen all I need to see."

Lorna walked over to the hunt board that held a dozen or so silver chafing dishes, then she lifted the covers one after another, pretending an interest in their contents. While she served herself a minute slice of ham and a spoon of mint aspic, Analise pulled Calvin aside and whispered in his ear. "If you have signed any papers, Calvin, Lieutenant Clement could sue you and Lorna for breach of promise."

At any other time, the wool merchant would have laughed aloud to think the empty-headed Analise Whidby was offering him legal advice, but at that moment he did not even smile. "Let him sue," he said. "My pockets are more than deep enough to stand the nonsense."

"But, Calvin. Only think of the scandal. Lorna's reputation would be ruined."

"Scandal be damned! This is my daughter's future we are talking about, and to put it plainly, I cannot like her intended or his family, be they ever so well connected." He lowered his voice, though it still carried across the room. "Now if it was his friend, Major Rutledge, that would be a different matter altogether."

"Good afternoon," said a deep, masculine voice. "Did I hear someone mention my name?"

As all eyes turned toward the parlor door, Stephen Rutledge entered the room. "I hope I did not keep you waiting."

Calvin Maitland was the first to speak. "Why, no. Not at all." Then a broad smile lit his face. "Come in, my boy. You are right on time."

When Lorna had heard the door open, she offered up a fervent prayer that the person joining them would prove to be Paul Clement. Her prayer went unanswered. Once again her fiancé had disappointed her, and once again she had cause to be grateful to Stephen Rutledge for his innate politeness.

As for the gentleman, when he came toward them and spied only three places set at table, he paused. "Do I intrude, Mr. Maitland? It would appear that I was not expected."

"Not in this room, perhaps. But have no fear, lad, for you could not be more welcome."

Stephen studied the older man's face for just a moment, then he bowed politely. "You are very kind, sir, to allow me to join your family party and share with you the company of two such beautiful ladies."

Though Lorna had once bid the major save his compliments for someone who might welcome them, her father obviously found nothing to dislike in the younger man's easy manners. "So, Major, you've an eye for the ladies, have you?"

"As to that, sir, a man would have to be blind not to admire such beauty as this."

The older man laughed. "True, lad. Very true. But come, allow me to make you known to Thomas's mother, Mrs. Whidby."

Analise curtsied prettily. "A pleasure, sir."

"*Au contraire,*" Stephen countered, a smile upon his lips, "the pleasure is entirely mine."

Naturally, Analise batted her long, dark lashes and smiled coyly. It was her typical reaction to admiration from a male, and it came as no surprise to her family. The thing that *did* surprise Lorna was the unexpected annoyance she felt when the major took Analise's hand and lifted it all the way to his lips, bestowing upon the slender fingers a totally improper kiss.

What impertinence! A true gentleman would never have kissed the hand of a lady he had only just met. Of course, the more Lorna knew of Stephen Rutledge, the more convinced she became that he cared nothing at all for gentlemanly behavior.

Or for the truth.

During the meal that followed, he told one whisker after another; all intended, Lorna presumed, for the amusement of Analise Whidby. Of course, Calvin Maitland was amused as well. He laughed so much that once he was obliged to wipe the moisture from his eyes and warn Analise not to be taken in by the military gentleman's Banbury tales.

Because her father's stay at Clement Park had not

been particularly pleasant, Lorna was quite happy to see him in good spirits. Unfortunately, she did not take a similarly liberal view of Analise's apparent enjoyment of the major's stories—possibly because the beauty insisted on laughing in that light, silly manner that one of her swains had once likened to the tinkling of a bell.

Tinkling of a bell, indeed!

"I vow, Major," Analise said, "your military exploits positively take my breath away. And though you see fit to jest about them, I am persuaded you were quite the hero while in the Peninsula. Like all our gallant lads, brave and valiant."

"Oh, I was, ma'am, I assure you. Of course," he drawled, "there was that night those gallant lads and I were to face Boney's troopes on the morrow."

He heightened the drama of his story by pausing to sip from his water goblet. "As you can imagine," he continued, "most of the men could not sleep for thinking of the coming battle, and those who might have slept were being kept awake by what sounded like the clicking of a hundred castanets.

"I will not sully your ears by repeating the angry words that noise provoked, but one of the men yelled into the darkness, wanting to know if there was a Spanish dance troupe in the vicinity.

" 'No,' replied another soldier in disgust, 'that noise you hear is caused by the quaking of the brave Major Rutledge's knees.' "

There was silence·for a moment, then everyone at the table burst out laughing.

"La, sir," Analise said, "you are a caution."

Lorna found she was not totally immune to the major's foolishness, and she, too, laughed at the picture he painted of himself quaking in his boots. Naturally, she did not believe a word of the story. She knew from the letters Paul had written her that the final campaign against Napoleon's army had represented days of suffering and unmitigated horror, and for her part, Lorna believed that all who had endured it were heroes. And their number included Major Stephen Rutledge.

While she pondered this truth, Lorna realized that the hero had spoken directly to her. "What? Oh, I beg your pardon, Major. I must have been woolgathering."

"I asked, Miss Maitland, if you were ready for tomorrow's trip to Stratford-upon-Avon. Mrs. Whidby informs me that she does not ride and will prefer to travel by carriage. What of you? If you should like it, there is a sweet-tempered little mare in the stable who should do nicely for a lady's mount."

Her father spoke before Lorna could answer. "My daughter is an accomplished horsewoman," he said. "She has a splendid seat. Oh, and remarkably gentle hands."

"That," the major said softly, "I can readily believe."

Lorna felt her cheeks grow warm. The way Stephen was looking at her, his dark eyes holding hers, she knew he was remembering this morning by the stream, when she had slipped her hand inside his collar to feel for his pulse.

"Rides as if born in the saddle," her father continued.

"You need say no more, Mr. Maitland, for I am convinced. And suitably impressed, I might add."

Wanting to put an end to this conversation about herself, Lorna said, "When listening to such effusive praise, Major, one must always make allowances for parental partiality."

Calvin Maitland admitted to a fair amount of partiality where his daughter was concerned, but he denied its influence in this instance. "Should you come upon a smooth stretch of land, Major Rutledge, and take it into your head to challenge my girl to a race, I beg you will not hazard more than a groat or two upon the outcome."

"Papa, please. I have no intention of racing anyone."

Lorna noticed a quite devilish light burning in Stephen's eyes, but only when they had finished the meal and were about to exit the breakfast parlor did she discover what had caused that light. He waited until that exact moment when her father and Analise had passed through the doorway, and he and Lorna were alone. When he spoke, his voice was low, the words for her ears only. "Bees. Horses. Is there no end to your talent? I find I have grown quite eager for tomorrow's outing, and that possible stretch of even ground."

Recalling the day she had arrived at Clement Park, and her first glimpse of Stephen astride that spirited gray gelding, Lorna was tempted by the possibility of pitting her skill against his. Some real exercise would be invigorating, and she would love to feel the sun on her face and the wind blowing through her hair, but most of all, she would like to see which of them—she or Stephen—could best the other.

Unfortunately, the thought had no sooner come to her than she remembered that her fiancé would be one of the party. She had no trouble imagining Paul's disapproval of such an unladylike competition, or the icy censure of her hostess, so Lorna shook her head, declining the challenge. "As I said earlier, Major, I do not intend to race."

"You cannot mean it, ma'am. How can you deny me that little pleasure? Me? A bona fide hero and—what was it Mrs. Whidby called me?—a 'brave and valiant' warrior."

Lorna put her hand to her ear, pretending to listen

to something in the distance. "What is that strange noise?" she asked. "I vow it reminds me of castanets. Is there a dancing troupe in the vicini—"

"Have a care, saucy minx, or I may be tempted to show you just what a dastardly fellow I really am."

She chuckled. "You would threaten me, sir? Here? In the presence of my family?"

He looked at her then, all teasing gone from his eyes, and that look sent a delicious shiver down Lorna's spine.

"That was no threat," he said, his voice low, his gaze resting provocatively upon her lips. "That was a promise."

Chapter Seven

The weather had been unseasonably crisp for the middle of May, but on the morning of the planned outing to the birthplace of Mr. William Shakespeare, the sun shone brightly and the sky was a beautiful, cloudless blue that seemed to stretch into infinity. It was just the sort of day Stephen most admired. Unfortunately, he had awakened with a feeling of disquiet—an uncertainty originating from his growing fondness for the Maitlands and his ever-increasing dislike of the Clement family.

Like other mornings here at Clement Park, he had allowed the footman who had been appointed his temporary valet to assist him to dress. Stephen had given up trying to convince the fellow that he did not need assistance, but he drew the line at having someone shave him. Some things a man must do for himself.

Once the night's growth was removed, he rinsed the remaining lather from his cheeks and let the footman hand him one of a pair of starched neckcloths. He needed only the one, and as soon as the linen was suitably arranged, Stephen donned a handsomely tailored waistcoat of smoke gray.

All the while he was dressing, he thought of nothing but the crumpled letter Lorna Maitland had hidden in the fallen willow tree yesterday morning. According to her missive, the lady wanted to know if her intended husband truly wished to marry her. Stephen would like to know the answer to that as well.

The question had kept him awake into the wee hours of the night.

Because of the letters he had exchanged with Lorna Maitland, Stephen felt partially responsible for her having agreed to a betrothal between herself and Paul Clement. For that reason, he had tried his best, without revealing the true authorship of the letters, to warn her not to go too gently into the proposed marriage.

She was an intelligent woman, and for such a person a hint should be sufficient. Still, Stephen had no way of knowing if she had given any serious consideration to his words.

It was not as if she *needed* to marry Paul Clement— or anyone else, for that matter. She had a doting father to protect her interests, and as his sole heir, Lorna had access to sufficient funds to secure for herself all the necessities and many of the elegancies of life. Her future comfort was guaranteed, with or without a husband. If she *chose* to marry, however, that was an entirely different matter.

Judging by her discarded missive, the lady was beginning to have real doubts about Paul's feelings. If that meant as well that she was doubting the wisdom of having agreed to a betrothal with a man she had never met, then Stephen had accomplished his mission in coming to Clement Park.

And yet, he was not satisfied—not completely. Something still niggled at his conscience, not letting him leave Lorna to her own devices. Unfortunately, he could not put a name to his feelings. Perhaps it was Paul's cool treatment of the lady

Deciding that was most likely the problem, Stephen had made up his mind to have a serious man-to-man talk with his comrade-in-arms. If Lorna should decide to continue with the betrothal plans, Stephen needed to know that he had done all within his power to ensure that Paul treated her with the respect she deserved.

He had tried to do so last evening. After another of those interminably dull dinners, where the repressive formality of the setting smothered all attempts at conversation, he had coerced Paul into accompanying him to the billiard room. "Where we might speak privately for a few minutes," he had said, "before joining the ladies."

At first Paul had not wanted to discuss anything having to do with his engagement, but Stephen had insisted. "Either you listen to what I have to say, Clement, and consider very carefully the suggestions I make, or I shall be forced to confess to Miss Maitland that it was I, and not you, who wrote her all those letters."

Judging by the haughty angle of Paul's handsome profile, he did not appreciate being spoken to in such a manner. He had said nothing, however, merely crossed the room to a burl wood cellaret, where he poured himself a rather large brandy. With his demeanor still icy cold and disinterested, he had taken the drink and settled himself into a red leather wing chair situated to right of the fireplace.

"Say what you must," he said at last, "and have done. I am listening."

Stephen did not take the other wing chair, for this was not to be a companionable talk between friends; instead, he leaned against the edge of the billiard table, his arms folded across his chest.

"I have it on good authority," he began, "that as a result of the letters I wrote to her, Miss Maitland has formed a sincere attachment . . . for you. She considers you her friend—one to whom she can speak honestly, without reserve—and in that spirit of honesty she wishes to know if you truly want to marry her."

"What foolishness is this? The matter is as good as settled. My mother has already sent the announcement of the betrothal to the papers, and nothing remains to be done but for the wool merchant to produce the wedding contracts that were agreed upon."

"Announcements and contracts notwithstanding, you have not answered the lady's question. Do you want to marry her?"

"I told you, the matter is as good as—"

"Nothing is settled. Trust me on this."

Paul swirled the brandy against the sides of the crystal, then he slowly sniffed the fruity bouquet of the distilled wine. He was about to take his first sip when Stephen repeated his question. "I ask you again—and I would like the truth—do you wish to marry Lorna Maitland?"

"Truthfully, Stephen, old man, what I wish is for this conversation to be at an end. It, and you, are becoming a dead bore."

"Perhaps, but if I were you, Clement, I would not be so quick to reject the importance of this conversation. Do not take the lady for granted, for she has a mind of her own. Furthermore, contrary to what Sir Duncan may have led you to believe about the wool merchant wishing to improve his social standing, Calvin Maitland is on the verge of quitting Clement Park and washing his hands of the entire idea of a betrothal between you and his daughter."

"What!" Paul nearly dropped the snifter, his manner no longer disinterested. "He cannot leave! Father needs that money to—" Whatever he had meant to say, he thought better of it and stopped himself, then downed the brandy in one large, angry gulp and threw the snifter against the centuries-old brick of the hearth. The delicate crystal smashed into hundreds of tiny pieces.

Silence followed the crash, then Paul slumped into the chair, his head laid back against the leather, his eyes closed. "I *must* marry her," he said finally.

The reply infuriated Stephen. While muttering an obscenity that only inflamed his fury, he pushed away from the billiard table, the thought crossing his mind that he would like nothing better than to grab Paul Clement by the collar, yank him from the chair, and throw *him* against the bricks.

At that moment, Stephen was convinced it would improve his temper no end to see Paul lying upon the hearth alongside the broken crystal. And yet, he willed himself to remain calm, to suppress his desire for punitive action. It might ease his own frustration to land the fellow a facer, but it would do nothing to ensure Lorna's future happiness.

Several minutes passed before he could speak with a semblance of composure. "If it is still your intention to marry the lady," he said, "then I have two suggestions. First, that you and your family stop treating the Maitlands as though they had been hired to clean the chimneys. And second, that you deal honestly with your fiancée and with her father."

Paul neither spoke nor opened his eyes, and Stephen could not be certain the fellow was even listening to him. Still, he had more to say, and he meant to say it. "You once told me that you had loved someone. Beatrice, I believe you called her. You said the lady chose another, and that as a result you no longer believed in love."

"Damn you, Rutledge. What is the point of this recollection?"

"The point is, I want you to see if you can remember how it feels to love someone who does not return your feelings."

"Of course I remember. The difficult part is to forget."

"Then if you have any humanity in your soul, do not make Miss Maitland suffer what you have suffered. If you have any affection for her, tell her so. On the other hand, if you do not think you could ever grow to care for her, then tell her that. She deserves to know the truth."

After a time, Paul had agreed to do as Stephen suggested. He had not, however, answered the question as to whether or not he *wished* to marry Lorna. That oversight accounted for Stephen's lack of sleep the night before and his continued disquiet this morning, but it did not account for the feeling he could not put a name to—the feeling that niggled at his insides and would not allow him to stop worrying about Lorna Maitland's happiness.

Stephen did not regret writing to her. Nor did he regret coming to Warwickshire to meet her. She was everything he had imagined her to be—a beautiful and kind-hearted woman, with a warm, passionate nature. And any man she chose to marry would be the luckiest man alive. *Damn his eyes!*

Not certain why his hands had balled into fists, or why he felt like using them on *the luckiest man alive*, Stephen reminded himself that he wished only good things for Lorna, including a life as full and sweet as the honey she gathered from her bees.

He had done all he could to warn her to consider her actions carefully, and now he had told Paul to be honest with her. He could do no more. So why did he not just walk away and get on with his own life?

It was all quite perplexing, especially since he had vowed after Waterloo never again to interfere in another person's affairs.

As a major in His Majesty's army, Stephen had the awesome responsibility of leading soldiers into battle. He gave the orders and his men were obliged to obey; they had no say in what were life-and-death decisions. It being war, some of those men had died as a result of Stephen's orders, and following the battle, he had sworn never again to usurp another person's right to choose his or her own course of action.

Like fine crystal, advice should be handled with care. It should never be passed around carelessly like cheap crockery.

As well, there was the matter of accountability. Stephen firmly believed that when one person took it upon himself to tell another how he should live his life, he had better be prepared to pick up the pieces should that person's world shatter as a result of the advice.

Accountability—was that the feeling Stephen could not name? The feeling that kept him here at Clement Park? Was it simply his sense of responsibility?

"Your answer, sir?"

Recalled to the present, Stephen stared at the footman turned valet. The man held a coat in either hand, and he appeared to have asked a question.

"What is it?"

"I wondered if you'd made your decision, sir. Is it to be the blue coat or the gray?"

Stephen pointed to the steel blue superfine, and while he worked his arms into the sleeves, he asked if the horses had been brought around to the front of the house.

"I should think so, Major. Sir Duncan sent word to the stable half an hour ago, instructing the grooms to saddle your gelding and the mare."

"Only the two?"

"Yes, sir. Lieutenant Clement has decided to ride

in her ladyship's landaulet with Mrs. Whidby and her son. He's not feeling quite the thing this morning, I'm afraid."

"Young Thomas? What ails the boy?"

The footman ran his finger inside his high collar as if the article had suddenly grown too tight. "The young gentleman is as fine as five pence, sir. It is the lieutenant who is . . . er . . . not at his best."

After their talk last evening, Stephen had left Paul in the billiard room, standing before the burl wood cellaret, the brandy decanter in his hand. The fool must have spent the evening there, drowning his sorrows. "Castaway, was he?"

"I fear so, sir. Lieutenant Clement had to be helped to his bed last night. The hour was late, and from what I hear, he was none too happy to be awakened this morning."

"I can believe it."

Stephen chuckled, feeling much better than he had a few minutes earlier. He may have lost a bit of sleep, but if he knew anything of the matter, Paul Clement was even now holding a throbbing head and praying for someone to run him through with a sword to put him out of his misery.

Good. The experience would not do Paul any permanent damage, and it might do Lorna a world of good to see her handsome Lochinvar appearing a bit green around the gills.

Eager to see how the gentleman's betrothed would react to seeing her fiancé at less than his best, Stephen accepted his hat from the footman and strode purposefully toward the bedchamber door. Even though he hurried down the corridor and took the stairs two at a time, his luck was out, for Paul and Lorna had both arrived at the portico before him.

Had he been there just two minutes earlier, Stephen would have been privy to Lorna's unvarnished opinion of her fiancé's condition. "I cannot believe it," she said. "He is jug-bitten!"

She and Thomas had come down the stairs together, each envisioning a day spent in discovery of new places and new faces. Arriving a bit earlier than expected, the cousins discovered more than they had anticipated. They, like the young groom who held the horses, watched in openmouthed amazement as Paul Clement's valet helped him into the landaulet.

"Deuce take it, Greeley!" Paul had muttered when he had stumbled onto the forward facing seat, and his curly brimmed beaver had fallen to the floor of the carriage. "Must you be so cow-handed?"

"Your pardon, sir."

"Where the devil is my hat?" Paul lifted his arm to shield his eyes. "Find it, you fool, before the light blinds me."

The valet reached inside the carriage and retrieved the hat, then after brushing it with his sleeve, he offered it to his master. "Here you are, sir. Good as new."

Without a word of appreciation to the servant, Paul snatched the hat and set it on his head, arranging it at an angle that would keep the painful sunlight from his eyes.

Sunlight. At the thought, Lorna recalled the letter Paul had sent her declaring his plan never to take the sun for granted again. "I shall treasure the sun's warmth more than gold," he had said.

Looking at him now, she wondered just how much he recalled of his own words.

What had become of the man who had written her such beautiful letters? And where was the handsome young man in the miniature?

The first time Lorna had set eyes upon Paul, he had stolen her breath away, for he had stood before a pair of long windows, and the afternoon sunlight that beamed upon his blond head had -put her in mind of one of Botticelli's angels. Could that have been only four days ago? The incident seemed a distant memory, and now no such angelic imagery occurred to her.

"Ah," someone said, "there you are. Good morning."

Even if she had not recognized the deep, pleasant voice, Lorna would have known it was Stephen Rutledge behind her. As always, she felt the vitality that seemed to radiate from him.

"Good morning, sir," Thomas replied. "It's a fine day for a drive."

"It is that, lad. Splendid weather, would you not agree, Miss Maitland?"

Lorna turned to reply, but when she saw Stephen standing in the doorway, looking strong and healthy and full of life—the very antithesis of the man in the carriage—the words died on her lips. She could do nothing but stare, admiring the pure masculinity of his features, the thick, dark hair that was brushed back from his angular face, and the sun-bronzed skin that glowed with that just-shaved look.

Without realizing she did so, Lorna breathed deeply, enjoying the clean, fresh aroma of his sandalwood shaving soap. He smelled wonderfully male, and Lorna had the oddest desire to nuzzle her face against his neck.

Taken aback by such an unexpectedly wanton thought, she turned quickly, pretending an interest in the little black mare that had been saddled for her use. "You were right, Major," she said. "The mare is a sweetheart."

"Her name is Cleopatra," Thomas informed him, "after the queen of the Nile. Cousin Lorna and I went to the barn earlier to give the mare an apple, and she ate it right out of my hand."

"Did she now? Since you appear to have all your fingers, I presume her manners were as dainty as a queen's should be."

"Quite, sir."

"I am happy to hear it, for had you been so foolish as to offer that apple to my gelding, we might even now be referring to you as Old Three Fingers."

At first, Thomas's eyes grew large with surprise, but when he realized the major was joking, he laughed with childish abandon. "Sir! You are the most complete hand."

"I am that," Stephen replied. "But my completeness notwithstanding, Thomas, I pray you will resist the temptation to call me Old Five Fingers."

At the major's joke, the boy went off into whoops. Even the groom in charge of the horses laughed aloud, and shielded by their merriment, Lorna was able to regain her composure.

They were discussing Cleopatra's alertness, and the way the little mare held her neck high and arched, when the entrance door opened and Analise stepped onto the portico, looking like a queen herself. Or perhaps a fairy princess was a more accurate description, for, as always, she was breathtakingly beautiful. The bright light revealed no flaws in her milky white complexion, and her dusky curls shone rich as sable beneath a chip straw gypsy hat, its taffeta ribbons perfectly matching the jonquil trim on her pale green curricle cloak.

Becoming very much the gentleman and protector, Thomas stepped to his mother's side and offered her his arm. "Lieutenant Clement is to go with us in the landaulet, Mama, because he does not feel well enough to ride."

Analise sent a darting glance toward the carriage, where the gentleman had slumped down in the seat, his face hidden behind his hat. "Oh, my," she said. "I pray he has not sickened from anything infectious."

"He's jug-bitten," the boy informed her. "Cousin Lorna said so."

Stephen raised one eyebrow, feigning surprise. "Your cousin said that, did she? And here was I, thinking only rough soldiers like me used such cant phrases."

Lorna felt her face grow red, but not wanting to give Stephen the satisfaction of seeing her blush, she hurried toward the mare and bid the groom toss her into the saddle.

After touching his cap respectfully, the servant bent down so Lorna could put her booted foot in his cupped hands. As soon as she had her balance, he straightened, and in one fluid motion tossed her up onto the mare's back. Once she was settled, the groom positioned her right foot securely in the stirrup, then she hooked her left knee over the leather-covered wooden pommel and wedged her left foot snugly behind her right calf.

While Lorna straightened the skirt of her blue habit so that her legs were discreetly covered, Stephen escorted Analise and Thomas to the carriage, where he spoke briefly with Paul. Whatever he said, the result was that Paul sat up straight and moved to the opposite seat so mother and son could sit together, facing forward.

Once the passengers were settled, Stephen nodded to the coachman, who cracked his whip above the heads of the matched grays. The pair were fresh and ready to go, and within seconds the landaulet was rolling up the carriageway toward the entrance gates.

Having seen to everyone's well-being, Stephen strode to the gelding, claimed the bridle from the groom, then slung his long, powerful leg over the equally powerful animal. "After you," he said, and

Lorna lost no time in tapping the little mare's neck with her riding crop and trotting off after the carriage.

The journey required at least two hours, and Lorna enjoyed every minute of it. By keeping to country lanes that wound past neatly maintained farms and the occasional cluster of small, half-timbered cottages, the riders were free to travel at a good pace, and they were also able to bypass the busy county town of Warwick, which was the halfway point.

It was marvelous to be out of doors on such a beautiful day, and Lorna found it equally pleasurable to be in the company of a gentleman who acknowledged her skill as a horsewoman by treating her not as a responsibility but as an equal.

For the first several miles, they had given the horses a good run, with neither rider trying to outdistance the other, and once the freshness was worn off the mounts, they reined them in from a gallop to a trot. Though Cleopatra responded immediately, like the lady she was, the gelding was not nearly so docile. Still, Stephen brought him around, using a firm but gentle hand to control the larger animal and keep him close by Lorna's mare.

For once the gentleman seemed to have relinquished his teasing ways in favor of the type of uncomplicated conversation that was possible while on horseback. "Your father was in the right of it, Lorna, concerning your talent for handling a horse. Judging by what I have witnessed, his partiality for you in no way impaired his discernment."

It was a sincere compliment, and Lorna accepted it graciously. "Thank you, Major. Coming from a seasoned cavalryman, that is praise indeed."

"Please. Would you do me the honor of calling me Stephen?"

Though Lorna was gratified by the easy camaraderie that had prompted the suggestion, she shook her head. "I could not do so, Major, for such familiarity would imply a relationship of much longer standing than you and I enjoy." When he looked as if he might argue, she added, "And do not think it passed my notice that you continue to use my name without so much as a by your leave."

"But I think of you as a friend. After all, you saved my life."

"I did nothing of the sort! And if you refer to the bee sting, I suggest that the less said about that incident the better."

He sighed as if much put upon. "Lorna—Lorna—Lorna."

"Major, I warn you, if you persist in—"

"Madam," he said, persisting despite her half-finished warning, "you told me once that you despised compliments, and I respected your feelings. However, if you continue in this cruel refusal to call me by my name, I shall have no recourse but to retaliate by telling you how beautiful you look in that blue habit."

If her cheeks grew warm, Lorna was honest enough to admit, at least to herself, that her embarrassment had nothing to do with despising the gentleman's very flattering observation. It had far more to do with the real reason why she had chosen to wear her old blue habit rather than don the green that had arrived less than a week ago from the modiste's in London.

She had told her maid that she preferred to wear the old habit because Analise would most likely be dressed in green. It was a falsehood. The truth of the matter was that Lorna had chosen the blue because the shade was known as gentian—the color Stephen had once likened to her eyes.

"What is it to be?" he asked. "Do you call me

Stephen, or must I sink to even more despicable acts?''

Not proof against his teasing, Lorna chuckled. ''I am not afraid of you, *Major Rutledge*.''

With the resigned look of one who has done his best to warn another, he said, ''Be it on your head then, when I wax poetic about the charm of your smile.'' He lowered his voice, and to Lorna's chagrin she found herself leaning forward in the saddle, the better to hear him.

''It is just a bit crooked,'' he said, ''and yet, utterly beguiling. Since most young ladies possess a looking glass, I assume you already realize that when you first begin to smile, the left corner of your mouth turns up just a moment before the right.''

Lorna had not been aware of that quirk, and though she professed not to care for compliments, she was honest enough to admit that it pleased her that Stephen had noticed such a small detail.

''It's a beautiful smile,'' he said just above a whisper, ''and a beautiful mouth. Perfectly formed for kissing.''

At his whispered words, Lorna felt an unexpected tingle in her lips—a tingle that was matched on every square inch of her skin. ''Sir, I—''

''And since you continue in your obstinacy, madam, I really must mention your complexion. No rose can hope to compete with the delightful warmth of your—''

''Enough! No more. I surrender.''

''You surrender, what?''

''I surrender . . . Stephen.''

He smiled at her then, and Lorna could not keep her gaze from resting upon his firm lips. Warmth coursed through every part of her body while she stared at his mouth, wondering if it, too, was perfectly formed for kissing. Somehow, she suspected it was.

Chapter Eight

To Lorna's relief, she was obliged to abandon her unruly thoughts about the kissableness of Stephen's lips, for the market town of Stratford-upon-Avon lay half a mile ahead of them, and they were no longer alone on the road. While she and Stephen paid special attention to their horses, keeping them on a tight rein to avoid colliding with a farmer's cart and a pair of smocked workmen who traveled on foot, Thomas turned around in the rear seat of the landaulet, stood on his knees, and began waving excitedly.

"Major!" he yelled, pointing at something in the distance. "See that water? It is the Avon River, and the coachman says that just beyond it is the Avon Canal. If you approve, he will stable the horses at the Talbot Inn, and from there we can take a short walk up the towpath to the locks. May we, Major?"

Because no one appeared to question the major's right to make such decisions, he cupped his hand around his mouth and yelled to the boy, "We will talk at the inn."

The town of William Shakespeare's birth was a popular place with visitors—both the elite and the not so elite. As the party from Clement Park approached the inn yard, Stephen spied dozens of these temporary citizens strolling about the cobblestone streets, peering into shop windows and cottage windows alike, all seeking to breathe the rarified air that had spawned the famous playwright and poet. As he soon discovered, the Talbot Inn was a favorite stopping place, and the innkeeper, a plump-faced, balding fellow in his middle years, happily played host to as many of the town's visitors as possible.

As a result, the sprawling, three-story, thatch-roofed building was alive with people and conversation. Regrettably, because of the glut of patrons, the innkeeper could supply the five newcomers with only one private room for the ladies, but he found space in the stables for the mare, the gelding, and the grays.

While the ladies refreshed themselves abovestairs, where a tray bearing tea and cakes was sent up to them, the three gentlemen visited the taproom. Desiring to set a good example, Stephen procured two glasses of sweetened lemonade—one for the boy and one for himself—but as he drank his portion of the tepid concoction, he watched with longing as Paul downed a tankard of their host's thick home brew.

Though Stephen feared the lemonade had left him with a permanent pucker, he was pleased to see that the tankard of ale had the happy effect of reviving Paul's body as well as his temperament. As a result, Paul was in much better spirits when the ladies joined them again.

As it turned out, when the entire party met in the inn yard, and a vote was taken as to their immediate destination, Thomas wanted nothing so much as to view the locks. Stephen and Lorna had no objection to escorting the lad to the canal, but his mother had less strenuous pursuits in mind.

"I have had enough of dust for the moment," Analise said, "and I should much prefer a leisurely stroll along the High Street, for a look-in at the shops."

"But, Mama, you can visit shops any day. If you

do not come with us to the locks, you will miss all the excitement."

His mother would not be persuaded, and because Paul had not recuperated sufficiently to wish to take part in a trek over a rough towpath, he offered to forgo ·the excitement of the canal as well. "I shall remain in the village with Mrs. Whidby."

Analise smiled prettily. "Why, how gallant of you, Lieutenant."

At a stern look from Stephen, Paul must have recalled their conversation of the night before, for he bowed in Lorna's direction. "Unless *you* wish my escort, Miss Maitland."

His fiancée blinked in surprise at this unlooked-for attention. "No, no. Not at all," she said, her cheeks quite pink with embarrassment. "What I mean to say is I should enjoy your escort, of course, but I will do quite well with Thomas and the major. You stay with Analise, and we will join you at . . . at . . ."

She looked up at Stephen, her expression asking him to complete the sentence for her. "At Mr. Shakespeare's birthplace on Henley Street," he said. "In three-quarters of an hour."

Stephen was not certain, but he thought the lady breathed a sigh. Was its cause relief? Or was it disappointment?

The plans made, Paul turned to Analise. "What say you, ma'am, to visiting that rather colorful church I spy just down the High Street." He pointed toward a splendid medieval structure whose blend of pink, fawn, and gray stonework glistened in the sun. "The innkeeper informed us that the stained glass window in the chancel is fourteenth century. A real treasure."

"It sounds quite pretty, sir, and I should like very much to see it. We can pause there on our way to the shops."

The expression on Paul's face was incredulous.

"Pause! But, ma'am, that window is . . ." Whatever he had been about to say, he thought better of it and bowed in a most gentlemanly fashion. "It shall be as you wish," he said, his tone resigned.

Without another word, he offered Analise his arm, and the handsome couple strolled in a leisurely fashion toward the ancient edifice. As for the more energetic trio, they lost no time in walking around to the rear of the Talbot Inn and finding the lane that led to the towpath and the locks.

Lorna soon discovered that Analise had been wise to choose the shops and the cobblestone streets of the village. As it turned out, the most direct way to reach the locks by foot involved a ten-minute walk up a steep hillside by way of a rough towpath, and the route proved more taxing than Lorna had expected.

The heavy barges that traveled the canals carried coal, produce, livestock, crates of furniture, and if room permitted, passengers. To get from one lock to the next, the barges had to be towed, and the power needed for that job was supplied by teams of shire horses led by young handlers who worked for the canal.

For years the oversized draft animals, with their heavily leathered legs, had traveled the towpath up and back, day in and day out, and not surprisingly, their massive hooves had worn into the hard-packed earth a trench some twenty inches deep. A person wishing to travel on the path had either to walk where the shires had walked, or attempt to balance himself on the narrow sides of the trench.

Lorna did not like either option. After she tried first the ruts and then the sides, stumbling and tripping until she thought surely she would break an ankle, Stephen took the choice from her by swooping her into his arms and carrying her the remainder of the way. Lorna had gasped and Thomas's mouth had fallen open, but Stephen had uttered not a single word; he simply continued on his way.

Stephen had not asked her permission to take such a liberty, but carrying her was an eminently practical solution. Lorna realized that immediately, which was why she raised fewer objections than might have been expected. As for her reaction to being swept off her feet, she was honest enough to admit—to herself, at least—that her feelings had nothing whatever to do with practicality.

When she was a child, her father had, on occasion, carried her up to bed to tuck her in. But as Lorna soon discovered, being carried by her father was not at all the same as being carried in the strong arms of a gentleman only six years her senior.

Thinking it would help distribute her weight, she slipped her arms around Stephen's shoulders. The gesture may have lessened the load for him, but it did nothing to calm the erratic beating of Lorna's pulse. Not surprisingly, being held against a man's rock-hard chest had set Lorna's heart to pounding. *Kerthump . . . kerthump . . . kerthump . . . kerthump . . .* it sounded like a child's ball bouncing down a flight of stairs, the beat so loud Lorna blushed to think Stephen might hear.

If he noticed anything, however, he was gentleman enough not to mention the fact. And for once, he seemed to have run out of teasing remarks. In fact, he was surprisingly quiet. When they reached the grassy knoll that encased the lock, he set her on her feet beside an ancient turkey oak, the only tree on the knoll, and only then did he look at her.

His right arm was still around her waist, to allow her a moment to get her balance, so their faces were quite close. As his dark eyes held hers, the seconds lengthened, and Lorna felt a current of some sort flowing between them, an awareness so tangible she felt she could reach out and catch it in her hand. Stephen felt it, too—she was certain of it—for his eyes darkened with some unreadable emotion. But before Lorna could discover what that emotion might be, he lowered his lids, effectively keeping his thoughts, whatever they were, to himself.

"Thank you," she said, the words all but sticking in her dry throat. "For . . . for carrying me over the rough spots."

He did not reply. He merely removed his arm from around her waist, stepped away from her, then inclined his head politely. After that he turned toward the canal, where he stared at the traffic on the muddy water as though he found barges loaded with produce and livestock fascinating.

Lorna could not emulate his calm. She was too unnerved by the jumble of feelings that continued to race through her body as a result of whatever it was that had passed between her and Stephen, and she felt a need to say something . . . anything. "I hope I was not too heavy."

Any other gentleman would have employed some time-worn platitude, possibly insisting that she was as light as a feather. But Stephen Rutledge was not any other gentleman; from him she expected a twinkle in the eye and a joking reply. To her surprise, she received neither. He continued to stare out over the water, the silence seeming to stretch between them.

Lorna was relieved when Thomas broke the silence by asking if he could go down close enough to watch the canal crew open the gate to the lock. "There is a barge waiting to be lowered to the next level," he said. "May I go closer?"

The boy's eagerness to view the coming event

made him positively quiver with anticipation. "Please say that I may, Cousin Lorna. Please?"

"Not by yourself," Stephen said. He put his hand on the boy's shoulder and turned him in the direction of the water, then without a word to Lorna, man and boy made their way down the knoll.

Twenty minutes were needed to complete the lowering of the barge—from the moment the single gate at the top of the chamber opened and the sluices began emptying the water, until the barge reached the bottom of the chamber and passed through the double gates. After that, another five minutes were required to tie the thick ropes from the barge to the team of shires, in preparation for towing the large craft to the next lock. Lorna had used that twenty-five-minute respite to regain control of her emotions.

Shafts of sunlight pierced the budding leaves of the turkey oak, dappling the grass where Lorna sat, her legs tucked beneath her, but she paid little attention to the patterns on the ground or to the sunlight. Instead, she reflected upon all that had happened to her in the past hour, recalling with particular interest the feel of Stephen's arms around her, and the way he had looked at her after he set her on her feet.

Then, of course, he had turned away. Had she done something to give him a disgust of her? Men were such perplexing creatures, and Lorna did not know what to think about Stephen's actions. If the truth be told, she did not know what to think about her own.

Who would have thought that a sensible woman would react like the veriest widgeon simply because a gentleman was polite enough to carry her across a bit of rough ground? Not that this was the first time that day she had acted like a simpleton. There had been that moment when Paul had surprised her by asking if she wished his escort to the lock.

Actually, Lorna had been more than surprised by Paul's question—she had been astonished. She had spent the past four days waiting for him to make an opportunity to spend time with her, and now, suddenly he had asked if she would like his company. Granted, his request lacked any real enthusiasm, but he *had* asked.

But why? And why now?

Lorna had come to Warwickshire for no other purpose than to spend time with Paul Clement—to see if she truly loved the man who had written her all those beautiful letters. When it appeared that Paul did not share her goal, she had been so bold as to ask him to come to her and had given him every opportunity to find her alone. He had not done so.

He had made no attempt to share a private moment with her. He had shown no interest in getting to know her. And his coolness, his indifference, had hurt her—hurt her more than she had wanted to admit.

And now, when she had all but decided that Paul was not the man she had believed him to be, he had offered her an olive branch.

Now, of course, she had to decide if that offer had come too late. Certain verbal commitments had been made between her father and his, but as yet there was no formal engagement. And in truth, Lorna had not thought of Paul once during the two-hour ride to Stratford-upon-Avon. It was as if she had forgotten his very existence. And why should she not? Especially when being in company with Stephen Rutledge had played such havoc with her senses.

"Cousin Lorna!" Thomas called. "Did you see it? Did you see the canal man turn the winding key that raised the paddles?" The boy was so excited he half skipped, half ran up the knoll toward her, leaving Stephen to follow at a slightly more decorous pace.

When he reached the spot where his cousin sat, his breath was coming in gasps, but he was too full of comments to spare the time to regulate his breathing. "Did you see the gate being pushed open? And the water emptying out of the lock? Did you see the way the boat went lower and lower until it reached the level of the canal?"

"Yes, I watched it all."

She might as well have saved her breath, or told him she flew away to the moon and missed the entire procedure, for Thomas described the mechanisms and their employment to her from beginning to end, as though she had not been there all along.

"Finally," he said, a full two minutes later, "after they opened the double gates below and the barge was completely free of the lock, the horse handlers let me pet the team of shires while they fastened the tow ropes. Did you see that, too?"

"Yes, of course I saw it," she lied. "How could I not? You were very brave to approach such large horses."

Thomas dropped to the ground beside her. "It was all so thrilling," he said. "The canalmen, the crew, the locks, the rushing water. Have you ever felt such excitement in your entire life?"

The honest reply would have been "Yes, when Stephen Rutledge held me in his arms."

Since that gentleman had reached the top of the knoll and now stood mere inches away, Lorna decided this was not the right time for honesty. Taking a page from the major's book, she answered Thomas's question with a jest.

"Have I ever felt such excitement before? Hmm. Let me see." She tapped her finger against her chin as if considering the matter. "There was that time the band of gypsies abducted me and took me to live with them in their caravan of colorful wagons. But no, now I think of it, that was not nearly as exciting as watching a barge being lowered in a lock."

"That is what I thought," Thomas replied.

Stephen laughed and reached out to assist Lorna to stand. "I fear your sarcasm was lost on the lad. But as for me, I found the story of your abduction by gypsies vastly exciting. One day you must share with me the entire adventure, as well as any other secrets you are keeping hidden behind that serene countenance."

After pulling her to her feet, Stephen did not release her hands immediately. He held them for a few moments in his, and the vitality Lorna felt flowing from his fingertips to hers left her feeling anything but serene. Still, she was happy that he had returned to his old teasing self.

They returned to Henley Street by a longer but less hazardous footpath that led from the back of the knoll; therefore, Lorna was quite able to walk without assistance. In fact, once they reached the cobblestone streets of the village, she feigned an interest in the displays in the shop windows, using that as an excuse to step ahead of the two males.

It was a cowardly thing to do—desertion, a cavalry man might say—but during the entire walk Thomas had rattled on endlessly about the locks and the canalmen, until Lorna thought she might scream. Without so much as an ounce of remorse, she had walked ahead, leaving Stephen at the boy's mercy, knowing, somehow, that he would never be unkind to a child.

Finally, Thomas had spied a fat yellow cat in the doorway of a wheelwright's shop, and he had ended his extolling of the locks so he might run ahead to pet the animal. The instant he left, Stephen stepped up beside Lorna. He said nothing, but the accusing, sidelong look her gave her spoke volumes.

Though she felt her lips quiver, Lorna managed to stop herself from smiling. "Tuppence for your thoughts," she said.

"Too expensive by half, madam. Furthermore, a woman with half a brain would not want to know what I am thinking."

She feigned innocence, batting her eyelashes in an exaggerated fashion. "Have no fear, sir, I can afford tuppence. Did you but know it, I have been known to go as high as sixpence for a really good thought."

Apparently unimpressed by her fluttering lashes, Stephen said, "I was planning a murder."

Lorna almost choked trying to suppress her laughter. "Oh," she said, batting her lashes once again. "Whose murder?"

Stephen gave her a telling glance. "Must you ask?"

Her answer was a chuckle. "And you an officer and a gentleman."

"Lucky for you, madam, that I am not still a member of His Majesty's army, or I should have you up before a firing squad, the penalty for desertion."

She laughed. "I shall consider myself fortunate to have escaped such a fate."

"Do not be so quick to laugh, for I have not totally given up the idea of exacting some forfeiture for your callous defection."

"Oh, I shall be quite happy to pay. What was my last offer? Sixpence, I believe."

He stopped walking and turned to look at her, and his lazy-lidded gaze sent a wave of sensations washing over Lorna's body. "Madam, the forfeit I had in mind had nothing to do with money."

He might have said more, but Thomas had returned. The yellow cat had allowed only a minimum of stroking, then apparently bored with the attention, he had sauntered off to the rear of the shop, leaving the boy alone and looking a bit dejected.

"I should like a dog," Thomas said to no one in particular.

Stephen heard the wistfulness in the seeming non sequitur—a wistfulness that revealed more eloquently than words ever could the extent of the boy's loneliness. During Stephen's ten years in the army, he had seen hundreds of lonely young lads—quite enough to recognize another one.

"What sort of dog would you like?" he asked, as though the boy had spoken directly to him. "I suppose you would prefer something rather large and fierce."

Thomas shook his head. "Any sort of dog would do. Even a small one. He need not be very grand or handsome, just as long as he liked me."

Stephen looked down at the freckled face. Poor Thomas, he thought. Had he no friends at all? Living in a spa town with a beautiful but empty-headed mother was no life for a boy. He needed a place to play—a place to run about and get dirt all over his nankeens—and he needed someone to play with.

"I know how it is to wish you had something," Stephen said.

"You do?"

"Certainly. Not two minutes ago your cousin offered me tuppence for my thoughts, and when you joined us, I had just begun telling her how much I would like to go fishing tomorrow." He sighed. "Of course, I cannot do it."

"Why not, sir. There are several places to fish at Clement Park."

"True, but having a *place* to fish is not the same thing as having a companion to share the experience. Call me peculiar if you will, but I have never liked to fish alone." He sighed again. "If only I had a friend who would go with me. Like your dog, he need not be very grand or handsome. He need not even be a grown person, just as long as he liked to fish."

Stephen said no more, and in just a moment he heard Thomas clear his throat. "Sir?" he said, his voice a bit hesitant.

"Yes, lad?"

"*I* like to fish."

"You don't say so!"

The boy nodded. "Really, I do."

"Well, now, if that is not a coincidence. And me wishing for just such a person. What say you, lad, shall we give it a try tomorrow?"

"Oh, yes, sir. I should like it of all things."

"Good enough. That is settled then. Tomorrow morning. Early. Just you, me, and the fishing poles."

When the boy smiled up at him, his blue eyes alight with pleasure, Stephen decided he had never had a nicer thank you. He was wrong.

A few moments later Thomas spied a mechanical bank in a shop window, and when he ran ahead to see the toy, Stephen felt Lorna standing close beside him. She hesitated an instant, then she slipped her arm through his. Both surprised and pleased by the unexpected gesture, he looked down at her, and the tenderness he saw in her eyes stole his breath away.

"You have a good heart," she whispered, "and I thank you, my friend."

Chapter Nine

As arranged before their trip to the locks, the trio met Paul and Analise on Henley Street, outside the home of John Shakespeare, his wife, Mary Arden, and the couple's ten children.

"There you are," Analise said. "The lieutenant and I have been waiting this age, and I began to wonder if you would ever get here."

"Mama," Thomas began immediately, "it was the most amazing thing. You should have come with us."

While the boy regaled his mother with all she had missed, Lorna moved closer to the two-story, half-timbered house that was the birthplace of William Shakespeare. Slowly, almost reverently, she reached her hand out and placed it against one of the wooden shutters at the corner window. "Oh, my," she whispered, awed by the significance of touching something the playwright had touched.

The unpretentious dwelling stood flush with a similar, though smaller, structure believed to be the building that had served as William's father's glovemaking shop, and though neither edifice was particularly handsome, Lorna felt a thrill just being near them. "It quite takes my breath away," she said, "to know that I am standing where the greatest writer of all time was born and reared."

She looked down at the cobblestones, almost as if

she expected to see Shakespeare's footprints. "How exciting to know he was in this very spot hundreds, perhaps thousands of times."

"Even more exciting," Stephen asked, "than being abducted by gypsies and taken to live in their caravan?"

"Philistine," she said. "Have you no reverence for greatness?"

"For greatness, yes. For cobblestones, no. But come, let us go inside the poet's house to see if there is anything within that will excite my Philistine's heart."

Lorna was more than happy to comply, but Analise was less enthusiastic. "We should have gone to Warwick," she said, "to see the castle. *That* would have been interesting."

"You may blame me," Stephen said, "for our not going to Warwick. But Miss Maitland can tell you, the trip to Stratford-upon-Avon was planned even before she arrived at Clement Park. I, that is, *we* thought she might like to see the Bard's birthplace."

Analise was not to be turned from her opinion. "But Warwick Castle is a magnificent structure, with grounds and gardens laid out by Capability Brown." She looked around her. "There is nothing here but a few insignificant shops and this shabby little house, which, by the way, smells of damp. And you will think I am making this up, Major, but they expect us to hand over a shilling each just to go inside the place."

"Ah," Stephen said, "a fellow Philistine."

Analise blinked her lovely green eyes. "Actually, sir, I was born in Kent. I have never even been to Fillsteen, but I am persuaded the place could not be less interesting than this."

Lorna gave Stephen a look that dared him to say another word, then she stepped beneath the small portico of the entrance. "You may, all of you, do whatever pleases you, but *I* wish to see the place where Shakespeare was born. And I do not consider a shilling too much to pay for the pleasure of doing so."

"Of course you would not," Stephen replied, "for if I recall, you were willing to waste as much as sixpence just to know what I was thinking."

A scathing retort sprang to Lorna's lips, but she was obliged to bite it back when Paul chose that moment to come forward and offer her his arm. "If you will, Miss Maitland, allow me to escort you inside."

Surprise silenced her tongue for several seconds, then she stammered something, what it was she did not know, but it must have served, for Paul opened the door and allowed her to precede him into the dim interior. Thankfully, once they were inside, Lorna's interest in the house made her forget everything else, including the novelty of being in company with her fiancé.

The walls of the smallish rooms had been painted in recent months, and most of the furniture on the ground floor had been built in the last century, at least two hundred years after Shakespeare's birth, but even those travesties could not lessen Lorna's enjoyment of the poet's home. Ignoring the furnishings, she went immediately to the steep, narrow stairs that led to the upper-story bedchambers. Once she stepped on the uneven wooden treads that were worn smooth from centuries of feet, she knew she had found what she sought. She lingered there, closing her eyes and trailing her hand slowly along the banister whose oak was almost black with age.

"Are you ill?" Paul asked.

The question irritated Lorna, for it obliged her to

open her eyes and explain her actions. "I was merely absorbing the essence of the place."

She must have betrayed her annoyance, for Paul stiffened. "Your pardon, madam. Pray, forgive the intrusion."

"No, no. It is I who should beg your pardon. I should not have spoken so sharply. Blame it, if you will, upon my admiration for the genius who once lived here."

"Of course," Paul replied, his voice still frosty. "Think nothing of it."

Unfortunately, Lorna thought of nothing else during the remainder of the tour, and her preoccupation with Paul's vexation robbed her of her enjoyment of the upper rooms. She had been rude, there was no denying that fact, and even though Paul said that he had forgiven her, the coolness of his demeanor gave the lie to his words. For that reason, Lorna spent the next half hour paying penance for her rudeness by trying to coax her escort into a happier mood.

When they were shown the bedchamber Shakespeare had shared with one or two of his brothers, Lorna took only a minute to look at the plain wooden four-poster bed and the much used washstand, both of which were most likely original to the house. Though she would have liked to linger, perhaps touch the counterpane upon the bed, she did not do so. Instead, she allowed Paul to escort her belowstairs and back out onto Henley Street, where they were soon joined by the rest of their party.

Stephen came immediately to her side. "Well, madam? Did the house live up to your expectations?"

"It did, sir. Especially the—"

"The stairway," he finished for her. "I know, I felt it, too. While climbing those stairs, I could almost believe that I had been transported to fifteen-sixty-four, and could hear the homey sounds of the ever-growing family as they went about their lives." He smiled then, albeit a bit sheepishly. "A bit fanciful for a Philistine, but there it is."

"Yes," Lorna said quietly, answering his smile with one of her own. "There it is."

The man who collected the shilling at the door had told Lorna that the home of Shakespeare's mother, Mary Arden, was the most charming of the houses open to the public. Unfortunately, that dwelling lay three miles to the west, in Wilmcote, and Lorna knew that Paul and Analise would not find it sufficiently interesting to warrant the trip. She was about to suggest they return to Clement Park when Stephen said they must, by all means, stop by Anne Hathaway's cottage.

Analise and Thomas had paused to admire the window where numerous important people who visited the Shakespeare house had signed their names upon the glass, so Paul was the only person present who objected to the plan to visit the Hathaway cottage. "I, for one, have seen enough," he said.

"Nonsense, old fellow. We cannot possibly leave Stratford-upon-Avon without viewing the childhood home of Shakespeare's wife. After all, she must have been quite dear to the poet's heart, for I understand that in his will he left her the second-best bed."

"What!" Lorna thought it another of Stephen's jests, and she told him she did not believe him.

"Madam, I am crushed that you should doubt my veracity. There is, of course, only one way to prove the truth of what I have told you, and that is to visit the cottage. I have it on good authority that a framed copy of the will is on display there."

Since the Hathaway cottage was in Shottery, scarce a mile from where they stood, everyone finally agree to go.

"But after that," Analise said, "we must return to the inn, for I vow I am famished from all this racketing about."

The path to the cottage allowed them to walk two abreast, and once again Paul fell into place beside Lorna. He did not offer her his arm this time, but he matched his step to hers, so that they remained side by side for the entire mile. Apparently he had forgiven her for her rudeness earlier, for he was not nearly as reserved as before. Still, it could not be said that theirs was a scintillating conversation.

"The weather was most cooperative today," he said.

"Yes, quite springlike."

"Sunny," he added.

"Yes," she agreed. "I had begun to think we were to go from winter to winter without any warm weather in between."

Obviously this observation required no response, for Paul said nothing more, and in hopes of keeping the conversation alive, Lorna called his attention to a handsome mulberry bush to their right. "I find the mulberry a most interesting bush," she said. "We have several of them at Epping Grange, and times out of mind I had seen the ripening fruit a veritable rainbow of colors. Green, yellow, gold, pink, crimson, black, all on the same bush at the same time. I find that quite remarkable."

"The fruit stains badly," he said.

There followed another silence, and after a time Paul said, "I collect that you said you liked to read, Miss Maitland. Do you enjoy the more feminine arts as well? Do you paint, or play an instrument?"

Lorna might have been pleased that he was showing even a little interest in her, had she not been surprised by the question. In fact, she looked up to see if he was in earnest. Surely he had not forgotten

the letter in which she had lamented her lack of pro-
ficiency at the pianoforte. He had commented upon
it in his reply, going so far as to say that her lack of
skill could never match his lack of discernment, for
he was as near to being tone deaf as made no difference. "A real tin ear," he had called himself.

She was about to remind him of his letter when
they rounded a corner and spied Anne Hathaway's
cottage. It was a respectable-sized dwelling with the
standard thatched roof and half-timbered walls, but
what gave the sturdy and well-preserved cottage its
charm was the hedge-enclosed garden filled almost
to overflowing with flowers, shrubs, and vegetables.

The inside of the cottage was not without interest,
furnished much as it had been during the courtship
of the eighteen-year-old poet and the woman who
was eight years his senior. But the hooded fireplace
and the hanging warming pans were not enough to
hold Analise's attention. As a result, the visitors remained at the cottage for less than a quarter of an
hour.

That was, however, quite long enough for Stephen
to produce the copy of the will. It hung from a nail
near the entrance door, and while Thomas and Paul
stepped out into the garden, Stephen removed the
frame document so Lorna might read it more easily.

She skimmed the closely written lines until she
came to the part about the second-best bed. "Shame-
less," she said. "One might almost think he meant
to insult her."

"Ah, well. To quote the man himself, 'The course
of true love never did run smooth.' "

"In this instance, I am inclined to think that was
the case." Lorna gave the will back to Stephen, and
he returned it to its place on the wall. "Did Shakespeare regret marrying her, do you think?"

Stephen lifted one dark eyebrow as if to suggest

that she already knew the answer to that question. "Marriages are not all made in heaven, you know."

"I suppose not. And yet, I cannot think of the Bard in any way but as a true romantic."

"So, regardless of the enigmatic bequest, you admire him still?"

"Yes. I am afraid I do."

"No matter the evidence of his possible meanness of spirit in dealing with his wife?"

"No matter the evidence," she said, then following his earlier lead, she quoted from *Two Gentlemen of Verona*. " 'I have no other but a woman's reason: I think him so because I think him so.' "

When Stephen and Lorna both laughed, Analise asked to be told what they had found so amusing in this unfashionable little cottage.

"Certainly not a marriage of true minds," Stephen said.

They were still smiling when Paul came to the door and once again claimed Lorna's attention. "Shall we go?" he asked, offering her his arm. "For my part, I have seen enough of plebeian antiquity for one day."

The host of the Talbot Inn was justifiably proud of his menu, and the five guests sat down to a nuncheon selection guaranteed to tempt the most finicky palate. Not that any of them suffered from that complaint. Within a very short time they were making their selections from a platter of well-turned venison, another of fricassee of hare, and bowls containing green peas and onions, boiled turnips, and sprouts served with a cheese sauce. There were also macaroons and golden seed cakes, a circumstance that appealed to Thomas, and no one left the table wishing for more.

"I wonder, lad," Stephen said, "if you would act as my aide-de-camp and take a message to the stables."

The boy squared his shoulders in the manner of a soldier and saluted. "Yes, sir, major. I am yours to command."

"Very well, soldier. Be so good as to tell the coachman that we wish to leave within . . ." His glance took in the other three adults. "Half an hour?"

They each nodded their agreement, then while the ladies went abovestairs to the private parlor, the gentlemen made use of the outdoor necessary located behind the inn. Stephen was the first to return to the inn yard, and as he rounded a corner of the stable, he spied Thomas crouched behind a rain barrel.

Thinking the lad meant to jump out at the proper moment and see if he could frighten one of the grown-ups into crying out, Stephen decided to turn the tables. He tiptoed very quietly toward the rain barrel, and when he was within a foot or two of the boy, he reached out and caught him by the collar of his jacket. "Ah, ha!" he said. "What have we here? A spy for the French? I vow, 'tis fortunate that I happened by, else we—"

Stephen stopped his foolishness immediately and released the boy's collar, for Thomas had grown quite pale. "Steady there, lad." Fearing the boy might swoon, he placed both his hands on the thin shoulders to offer support.

To his surprise, the boy threw his arms around Stephen's waist and held him tightly, all the while his reed-thin body shook with fright. Feeling like an ogre, Stephen said, "Forgive me, Thomas. It was but a jest, and obviously a poor one. When I saw you hiding, I thought you meant to play a trick on us, and I . . . well, never mind what I intended. It was badly done and I beg your pardon."

"No, no," Thomas said. "It was not you. I . . . I thought I saw someone."

There was no doubting the boy's sincerity, and Stephen asked him whom had he seen and where.

"In the stable," he said. "A tallish man in a brown coat and gold waistcoat. He has red hair, and his name is Felix Treherne."

"Who is he?" Stephen asked.

Thomas merely shook his head, indicating that he would not tell, and Stephen was obliged, for the moment at least, to honor the youngster's wishes. In any event, he told Thomas to wait there while he had a look in the stables. "Will you do that?"

"Yes, sir."

As it turned out, Stephen discovered four men in the stable, all of them young ostlers who worked for the inn. And not one of them possessed red hair.

After questioning the ostlers, who swore to a man that they had seen no one lurking about, Stephen returned to the rain barrel, where young Thomas waited. "I found no one who fit the description you gave, lad. Are you certain you were not mistaken? It is rather dark in the stable, and anyone might be forgiven for thinking he saw something when he did not. Could it have been a shadow, do you think?"

"P . . . perhaps." His voice sounded more hopeful than convinced, and after a moment he said, "Major, could we . . . that is, do you have to tell my mother what happened? She would be frightened."

"I shall tell no one, if that is your wish. Word of a gentleman."

From the fright he had seen in the boy's eyes, Stephen did not doubt for one moment that Thomas Whidby had seen what he reported, and it was no shadow. Furthermore, the person he saw had something to do with the lovely Analise, and might even pose a threat of some kind. For the moment he would ask the boy no more, but he vowed to keep a close eye on the Whidbys, mother and son, and at some more appropriate time, he would discover who had frightened the lad, and why.

Chapter Ten

Lorna would have liked to let the horses have their heads for a few miles of the return trip. Now that they were well outside Stratford-upon-Avon, the lane was relatively flat, and aside from the party from Clement Park, there were no other travelers about. It was a perfect stretch to test their mettle, but when she suggested to Stephen that they see who would be first to reach the next village, he declined the offer.

"If you are afraid of losing your money, sir, we need not wager."

"You say that now, madam, but upon the highly unlikely event that you should precede me into the village, I—"

"Highly unlikely! A sure thing, more like."

"As I was saying, in the event you should prove the better rider, I have no doubt you would claim we had agreed upon some quite exorbitant amount. Females, I have discovered, do not treat wagers with the seriousness they deserve. If they lose, they will vow they were teasing the entire time. But let them win, and they insist the wager was indisputable. Either way the poor man loses."

"Poor man, indeed. Had you not just returned from years of military duty, I might be misled into thinking you were afraid of me."

"Oh, but I am, madam. Terrified. Where the ladies

are concerned, we hapless males have not a fighting chance."

Fighting chance or no, Lorna could not persuade Stephen to spur the horses to any pace faster than a trot. All her arguments seemed to fall on deaf ears. Once or twice he glanced over his shoulder toward the landaulet, and if Lorna had not known it to be a foolish idea, she might have supposed that he wished to remain close to the carriage. Though why that should be the case, she could not say.

Unless, of course, Stephen had succumbed to Analise's charms.

The dusky-haired beauty might declare that she did not care for young men, but Lorna had noticed that she never missed an opportunity to bat her lashes at them, or tell them how *wonderful* she thought they were. As for Stephen, Lorna had thought he liked women with a bit more intelligence. She had even flattered herself that he admired that quality in her, and it was a rather lowering thought that he might have become one of Analise's conquests.

Moments ago, Lorna had felt quite happy. It had been a truly lovely day, and now, suddenly, she felt a heaviness settle in her chest—a sad feeling she could not explain.

"Fricasseed hare," she muttered, happy to have solved the mystery.

"I beg your pardon?"

"Nothing, sir. I was thinking aloud."

"A dangerous habit, my friend. People might mistake you for a Bedlamite."

"As to that, I am afraid your warning comes too late, for they already do."

"You are not serious."

"Oh, but I am, sir. Quite serious. Judging by the strange looks I get from many of our neighbors in

Plemstock, those worthies find my behavior question-
able at best."

Stephen looked at her as though he could not decide if she was in earnest. "I find that difficult to
believe, for you are the sanest person I ever met."

Lorna had no idea how she should respond to
being called sane. She suspected it was meant as a
compliment, but since she could not be sure of it, she
chose to say nothing in response. Instead, she strove
to explain her neighbors. "Look at it from their per-
spective: There must be *some* reason why a woman
with a handsome dowry has reached the age of five-
and-twenty without being married."

"Ah, yes. I see your point. There could be no other
explanation for your single state, save lunacy."

Lorna chuckled. "I will admit that my decision to
become a beekeeper added fuel to that particular fire.
In fact, according to the vicar's daughter, who is my
dearest friend, that one piece of information alone
kept the gossips dashing from house to house for at
least a month."

Stephen took another quick glance over his shoulder at the landaulet, then he returned his attention
to Lorna. "I had wondered," he said, "how you came
to be an apiarist. But you may keep the answer to
yourself if you mean to fob me off with tales of baying at the moon."

"Oh, no. I have never bayed at the moon. Gazed
overlong, perhaps, but never bayed."

"I am relieved to hear it. Now, about the bees."

Before this moment, no one had ever asked Lorna
that question. When she stocked the first skep, the
servants at Epping Grange had *tsk-tsked* and shaken
their heads, and her father had bellowed that beekeeping was no hobby for a lady—especially a
Whidby lady—but no one had ever asked her
reasons.

"They do not weigh as much as a sheep," she said.

"Excuse me?"

"Bees," she said, "weigh only a few ounces. And pound for pound, so to speak, they produce more food than any other animal."

"I see," Stephen said. "And before you discovered that interesting fact, were you toying with the idea of raising sheep?"

"Oh, no. That notion would have had my father baying at the moon! It was one of the village women who wanted to raise the sheep. And she might have done so, except that she is approaching her ninetieth year, and is no longer able to lift heavy objects."

Stephen waited until they had safely guided the horses around a large birch limb that overhung the lane, then he said, "If it was your purpose to pique my interest with this tale of sheep and elderly villagers, you have done so. Now, I wish you will get on with the story before I lose my patience and throttle you."

"You have patience?" she asked. "I had not noticed that about you."

"Madam," he said, a warning tone in his voice.

Judging it prudent to begin her story, Lorna said, "The elderly lady lost her only son to influenza, and she needed some occupation that would allow her to support herself. Papa helped her as much as she would permit, but she was far too proud to accept charity indefinitely, so after she and I discussed the matter at some length, we decided that keeping bees was the logical solution."

"Not that I doubt your logic, but how did you arrive at that conclusion."

"It was simple, really. Bees could be useful to the woman in two ways. First, she could sell the honey and the wax, and second, she could sell her services to the farmers by taking her skeps to their orchards and letting her bees pollinate the farmer's fruit trees."

Stephen nodded his agreement with her rationale. "That explains the elderly woman's reasons for becoming a beekeeper. But it does not explain yours."

"It is quite simple, actually. *I* had to learn how to handle the bees so I could teach her."

"Naturally," he said, his tone droll. "How foolish of me not to have guessed as much. And once you learned, and the elderly woman learned, why did you continue? Is the occupation so riveting?"

She paused for a moment, and Stephen thought she meant not to answer, but he was mistaken. "Bees are quite fascinating creatures," she said, "and anyone might enjoy observing them, but it was the returning soldiers who kept me stocking more and more skeps."

Stephen had thought her story disjointed before, but the mention of soldiers seemed a total non sequitur. "Pray, madam, what have returning soldiers to do with bees?"

"A great deal. Many of the soldiers returned from the battlefields with broken bodies, and once they discovered that there were no jobs for men with only one arm or one leg, their spirits became broken as well. When I saw these injured men walking the lanes, seeking work and finding little, it occurred to me that if an elderly lady could support herself by keeping bees, the same might be true of these poor men."

"So you taught them as well."

"A few of them. Some of them were not interested, and others were too afraid of being stung. If you would keep bees, you must overcome that fear. And, of course, there is the time factor."

"Time factor?"

She tapped her forehead with her finger, as if to

imply that he should think first before asking a silly question. "Bees do not create new colonies overnight, and I must wait until the time is right to introduce them to a new skep. For that reason, I keep a half dozen colonies at all times, and each time a new skep is established, I notify one of the ex-soldiers that his bees are ready to be taken home."

Stephen listened to her story with twofold interest. On the one hand he found it amazing that she had come upon a simple solution to what was a complex problem, and on the other hand he was fascinated that she had absolutely no idea how unselfishly she had behaved.

He had liked Lorna Maitland from the first letter he had read, and over the months, as their correspondence had grown, he had come to admire her intelligence and her common sense. But until this moment, he had not known of her compassion. She had seen a need and had supplied it; not by giving a handout, but by providing honest work.

"The poor are always with us," he said. "What made you choose to help the soldiers?"

She did not look at him, but at the mare's sleek black neck. "I chose to help them," she said softly, "because I knew from Paul's letters the sacrifices these men had made for their country. And," she added, her voice quiet, almost shy, "because the man I loved was a soldier, one who was still making a soldier's sacrifice.

"You will think me foolish, sir, but by helping the soldiers I met, I hoped that I might, somehow, be making life just a bit easier for the man I loved."

The remainder of the ride back to Clement Park was completed in relative silence, though not a companionable silence. Stephen appeared preoccupied with his thoughts, and Lorna traced his lack of conversation to the instant she had told him of her love. She wished now that she had kept still. Obviously the topic was too personal. Why else would Stephen have erected this invisible wall of reserve?

She was almost happy to see the carriageway at the Park, and as the mare and the gelding galloped across the limestone bridge that separated the ponds, Lorna wondered if she would ever understand men. She had thought she and Paul were friends—had been friends for a year—then she had met him face-to-face, and his every word, his every action had been so cool toward her that she and he might as well have been complete strangers.

Now, here was Stephen behaving in an inexplicable manner. Though Lorna had not known of his existence until a few days ago, she had felt a rapport between them almost from the first day they met. Judging by their easy camaraderie, she had every reason to believe he looked upon her as a friend. Now suddenly he was treating her with reserve.

Had her common sense gone lacking, or did the fault rest with the two men?

She could not shake off the niggling feeling that there was something at work here, some piece of information that had been withheld from her. What that piece of information might be, Lorna could not even guess, and the unanswered question left her feeling irritable. For that reason, the instant she reached the front portico she allowed the groom to assist her to alight, then she hurried into the house, sped through the vestibule without so much as a nod toward the footman who had opened the door, and ran up the stairs that gave access to her bedchamber.

Though she knew she was being rude, perhaps even childish, at that moment Lorna did not care. Let Stephen and Paul wonder about *her* behavior for a change!

To her annoyance, she had been in her bedchamber only long enough to toss her gloves and riding crop onto the small satinwood dressing table when a knock sounded at her door. "Blast! In a house this size, a person ought to be able to find a bit of privacy."

When she did not answer, the knock sounded again. "Miss?"

It was the young parlor maid who was acting as Lorna's temporary lady's maid. "Go away, Bess. I do not need your services just now."

"If you please, miss. I've a message for you from her ladyship."

Lady Clement was the last person Lorna wished to think of at that moment. "Come back later. I am persuaded the message will wait."

"Please, miss." The girl's voice had a husky quality, as though she might be close to tears. "Let me in, do, else Mr. Simmons will have my hide."

Mr. Simmons, indeed. Lorna would have liked nothing better than to put a few well-chosen words into the ear of that pickle-faced snob of a butler, but she had been mistress of her father's house for too many years not to understand the pecking order observed by the servants. Any satisfaction she derived from venting her spleen upon the butler would ultimately find its way down to the young maid, who might be dismissed from service.

With a sigh of resignation, Lorna called, "Enter."

The girl scurried into the room and closed the door behind her. After bobbing a curtsy, she thanked Lorna profusely for not sending her away. " 'Twere ever so kind of you, miss. Mr. Simmons would've turned me off for sure."

"Yes, well, give me the message, Bess, then allow me some privacy. I wish to be alone."

The girl bobbed another curtsy. "Yes, miss. A rest

is just what you need. I can wake you in plenty of time to dress before the guests arrive."

"Guests? What guests are you talking about?"

"That's the message I was to deliver, miss. Her ladyship has invited a few of the neighbors to come make your acquaintance."

A week ago Lorna might have taken pleasure in the prospect of meeting her fiancé's neighbors, but at that moment she could not imagine anything she wanted to do less. "How many are invited? Do you know the number?"

"Not to worry, miss. There'll be only them as are suitable. Her ladyship don't hobnob with just anybody."

Lorna had no trouble believing that. "An approximate number then."

"I can't rightly say, miss. Upwards of a dozen guests will sit down to dinner, and another dozen or so will come later for tea."

"What! Two dozen?"

" 'Course, I can't be sure. Last I heard, not all the response cards had been received."

"Response cards?" Lorna's mouth was suddenly dry as dust, and she was obliged to swallow before she could speak again. "I had assumed this was some sort of impromptu dinner party."

"Oh, no, miss. Lady Clement don't give none but formal parties."

"But why? What I mean is, why now?"

"As to that, miss, I'm afeared I don't know."

"Of course not. How could you? The question was meant for myself."

The maid glanced toward the closed door, as if to assure herself that no one could overhear. " 'Course," she said, "you been so nice to me, and all, I reckon it wouldn't hurt none if I told you what I heard."

"No, really, Bess. There is no need."

Already warming to the subject, the servant continued. "There were an argument last night. Now back home, my mam and pap fight all the time, and us young 'uns too. B'aint nothing unusual about that. But it's different here. Her ladyship and Sir Duncan they always speak quietlike, so all us in the servants' hall were surprised to know they were arguing with Lieutenant Clement.

"The shouting went on for a long time, and it didn't end 'til the lieutenant stormed out of the blue drawing room, slamming the door behind him. Shouting, he was, sommit about it were not his fault the sheepherder were planning to take his gold and leave."

Lorna stiffened.

"Not that I know what he meant by that, miss, for there b'aint no sheep at Clement Park, and no sheepherders neither."

The girl continued with her story, but Lorna was too stunned to hear any but the last few remarks. "According to Miss Gaines, her ladyship's dresser, her and Lady Clement spent the rest of the night writing out the cards of invitation."

Lorna bit her lip to force herself to remain calm. The tactic did not work, for her heart jumped into her throat as though it meant to take up residence. "You are sure of this, Bess? You are not mistaken about any of this?"

"No, miss, I'm not mistaken. Mr. Simmons sent two of the footmen out this morning to deliver the cards. Early it was, even before you and the other guests left for Stratford-upon-Avon."

Lorna tried to swallow the gigantic obstacle that threatened to choke her. She had known from the beginning that her dowry played a part in this betrothal, but she had always assumed the money meant no more to Paul than it did to her.

"Stupid! Stupid! Stupid!"

How could she have been so naive? When a man is as wealthy as Calvin Maitland, his daughter must always appear as the logical route to his money.

Something, or someone, had frightened the family into believing that her father was close to backing out of the arrangement. But who? Not her father, for he would never renege on his promise to Lorna to wait until she had come to some sort of understanding with Paul.

Be that as it may, someone had meddled in her life, and the result was that Lady Clement had taken it upon herself, without so much as a word to Lorna, to force the issue.

The woman was no fool; she must have known that invitations to such a hurried affair would arouse all manner of speculation, especially invitations to the type of formal affair she had planned. There could be no question as to what the neighbors would be expecting to hear at Clement Park this evening.

"Bess," she said, her voice none too steady. "Do you know where my father is?"

"Y . . . yes, miss. He's in the billiard room, reading the London papers what arrived this morning with the post. You want I should fetch him for—"

The maid halted mid-sentence, for the young lady had suddenly gathered up the skirt of her riding habit and run from the room, throwing the door open so fast it crashed against the bedchamber wall.

"Papa!" Lorna said, the instant she entered the billiard room. "Do you know what Lady Clement has—"

"I know," he said. His face was devoid of all emotion, but the quiet tone of his voice told his daughter that he was livid. "The moment I read it, I knew it was her put it in. Sir Duncan may think himself bet-

ter nor me, but he's not stupid enough ter do this
without my approval."

Even in her agitated state, Lorna realized that she
and her father were speaking of two different of-
fenses, for Calvin Maitland held the *Times* in his
hand, his strong fingers crushing the pages. "You
said you read something, Papa. What was it?"

When he did not answer, Lorna reached out and
caught hold of the mutilated newspaper. "Let me see
it," she said.

Bowing to the inevitable, her father allowed her to
take the paper from his fingers, then he waited quietly while she skimmed over the various articles.
Near the bottom of the page, listed under announcements of recent betrothals, Lorna found the three
harmless-looking lines. "No," she said. "No. No. No.
No. No."

As if unable to stop herself, she read the notice
aloud. "Lieutenant Paul Clement of Beddingford,
Warwickshire, to Miss Lorna Maitland of Plemstock,
Oxfordshire. A summer wedding is planned."

The words, though quietly spoken, seemed to echo
in the room, and Lorna heard them as if they had
been read by someone else, someone whose voice she
did not even recognize.

"They do not even like me," she said at last.
"None of them. Neither Paul nor his parents." The
humiliation of such an admission made Lorna's voice
catch in her throat, but she breathed deeply until she
had her emotions under control. "Since they are not
overly fond of me, I wonder what, or who, prompted
them to do this?"

"Who can say, lass."

Lorna read the announcement through again, as if
to assure herself that her eyes had not played her
tricks, then she walked over to the brick hearth and
tossed the newspaper into the fire. The bright orange

flames consumed it within a matter of seconds. "Now," she said, "I wish you will tell me, Papa, what on earth I ought to do."

Her father joined her at the fireplace, where he placed his hands upon her shoulders and turned her to face him. "Before I answer that, lass, I've one question. I believe you fancied yourself in love with Lieutenant Clement. Do you still feel the same?"

Lorna shook her head. "I was in love with the Paul Clement who wrote me those warm, tender letters. The Paul Clement I met here is not that man. What happened to make him change, I do not know. Perhaps it was the war, or perhaps it was returning to his normal life. Whatever the reason, I do not like the man I see."

"You've no wish to marry him then?"

"No. I have no wish to marry him. Though how I am to get out of this abominable affair without becoming fodder for the gossips, I do not know."

"Let me handle this, lass. No need for you ter trouble yourself. I've a strong back and a tough hide, and nothing Sir Duncan, his lady, or anyone else says will distress me."

"Papa, I cannot allow you to do this alone."

"And why not, I'd like ter know? The blame is mine. 'Tis I who first listened ter the scheme of a marriage between you and Paul Clement. If I'd not told you of it, if I'd kept my mummer shut, we'd neither of us be here now."

"You meant it for the best, Papa. You wanted me to have a home and family, and, in truth, I wanted those things for myself."

"Aye, lass, but it was me that was blinded by the glitter of a title." He hesitated for a moment, and when he spoke again, his throat was husky with emotion. "I wanted you to have the sort of life you deserved . . . the sort of society your mother gave up when she married a man in trade."

"But Mother loved you. She was happy with her choice. Surely you never believed she regretted marrying you?"

When he said nothing, Lorna put her arms around her father's neck and laid her head against his shoulder. "No one could have been a better husband or a better father than you. And you may believe me when I tell you that Mother never wanted any society but yours."

"You're sure, lass?"

"Positive. Just as I am certain that I have the best, the kindest father in all the world. And if I could have three wishes, I would use them all to help me find a man I loved and respected as much as I love and respect you."

Calvin Maitland gave his daughter a hug that threatened to crush her ribs, then he put her away. "Now, now. That is enough of that. I've too much ter do ter be wasting time standing here talking foolishness."

"Yes, Papa Bear."

Her father ignored her impudence and straightened the neckcloth she had mussed. "I've been thinking on what we should do about this announcement, and I'm convinced that you should let me deal with it. I'll write my lawyer first thing tomorrow, and—"

"But you do not know the whole. Lady Clement has sent out invitations for a party. For tonight. And I do not need to tell you what she thinks to accomplish by such a move."

"The witch!"

"I could not have expressed it better myself. It is obvious that Paul's mother believes she can intimidate me into formalizing the engagement and going through with the wedding."

Calvin Maitland swore beneath his breath. "She thinks you will agree just ter avoid a scandal."

"She will soon learn the error of that assumption."

"Aye, that she will. And she'll learn, too, that Calvin Maitland is not a man ter be manipulated by a haughty female who thinks herself better than him and his family."

He reached over and pinched Lorna's chin as though she were still a child of ten. "You go up and have a nice leisurely soak, there's a good girl, then climb into bed. Tell your maid you've the headache, and bid her bring your supper on a tray. No need ter come down ter face her ladyship's guests."

"You would have me play the coward, Papa?"

"Never, lass."

She took one of his rough hands between hers and bid him remember that she, too, was a Maitland. "Regardless of the impropriety of sending that announcement, the Clements are still our hosts. We are guests in their home, and I, for one, intend to show them what *real* manners are. I will go to their party. I will smile at their guests. Then tomorrow I will pack my bags and leave Clement Park, never to return."

At first Lorna thought her father meant to protest, but whatever his reservations, he agreed to do as she asked. "And what of the lawyer?" he asked. "Preliminary agreements were reached, and the legalities will still need ter be addressed."

"I know, but I beg you will delay dealing with the legalities until we are returned to Epping Grange. For tonight, at least, let us say nothing."

"If that is the way you want it, that is the way it will be."

"Thank you, Papa. No matter what is said, or even hinted at, you and I are agreed—are we not?—that we will neither confirm nor deny anything."

Her father nodded. "You have my word on it. It will go hard with me to keep a civil tongue in my head when face-to-face with Sir Duncan and Lady Clement, but for the time being I will forgo the pleasure of telling our hosts what I think of their high-handed tactics. As for the party guests, no matter what they ask, I'll neither confirm nor deny an engagement between you and Paul Clement."

Lorna squared her shoulders, as if readying herself for the coming battle. "Getting through this evening will not be easy, nor will it be pleasant. But I mean to behave in a ladylike manner. If Lady Clement's guests wish to gossip, they will have to make do with what her ladyship has said and done. I realize that they will eventually call me a jilt, but I will not give them reason to say that a Maitland was ill-bred."

Chapter Eleven

Stephen rested his neck against the rolled-up towel, then closed his eyes, hoping the steam of the bathwater would soothe his troubled thoughts, perhaps wash away the sound of Lorna's voice. A full two hours had passed since their ride from Stratford-upon-Avon, and he could still hear her words, still see her serious expression. "By helping the soldiers I met," she had said, "I hoped that I might, somehow, be making life just a bit easier for the man I loved."

The man she loved. Damnation! After nearly a week in company with that icicle on legs, Lorna still fancied herself in love with Paul Clement.

Could she not see that she deserved better?

Lorna Maitland was kind and warm-hearted, and the most beautiful and desirable woman he had ever met. She deserved a man who loved her to the depths of his soul, not some lout who possessed a handsome face with nothing behind it. She deserved a real man—one who would show her the mysteries of life. A man who would take her in his arms and carry her to his bed, where he would awaken the passion that was within, just waiting to bloom and be shared.

That was what she deserved, but what was Stephen to do about it? If Lorna loved Paul, what more was there to say? Stephen had done all he could to—

"No! Deuce take it! There is one more thing I can do."

His mind made up, he stood, and in his haste he sloshed soapy water all over the fine Axminster carpet. Not that he cared one whit about the spilled water or the wet footprints he left when he stepped over the side of the iron tub. He had more important matters to consider—matters that concerned Lorna Maitland's future happiness.

Hurriedly Stephen wrapped a thick terry bath sheet around his hips, then still dripping water, he crossed the room to the Sheraton rosewood writing desk. After lifting the top, he removed a stack of vellum, a quill, and a leather-covered ink pot, then pulled out the writing slide and seated himself in the ladder-back chair. He delayed only a matter of moments to compose his thoughts, then he dipped the stylus in the ink and began to write.

For the better part of an hour, the only sound in the bedchamber was the steady scratching of the stylus across the paper. Finally, after he had filled five pages, Stephen tossed the quill upon the desk. He folded the sheets, sealed them with a wafer, then leaned back in the chair. "Now," he said, "I have done all I know to do."

When Lorna returned to her bedchamber to dress for the evening, she spied the letter that had been propped against the looking glass on her dressing table. The letter was from Paul; she recognized the handwriting. She had received enough of his letters to know his writing even at a distance.

At Lorna's entrance, the young maid, who sat in the corner by the window, waiting to help her dress for the party, stood and bobbed a curtsy. She must have noticed Lorna looking toward the dressing table, for she said, "One of the footmen brought the letter, miss. He said I was to see you read it without delay."

Lorna remained where she was. When she did not move toward the dressing table, Bess asked, "Shall I fetch the brace of candles from the mantlepiece, so you can see to read your letter?"

"Thank you, no."

"But the footman said—"

"It can wait."

Lorna had read just about enough from the Clement family for one day, and she had no interest in anything Paul had to say. Not now. Not when she was so angry she wanted to scream and toss furniture against the walls.

At that moment she wanted nothing so much as to be alone. She needed solitude in which to think, so she bid the maid go belowstairs to fetch her a cup of tea.

"But, miss, there is scarce an hour until the dinner gong sounds, and—"

"A cup of tea, Bess. If you please."

The servant curtsied. "Yes, miss. Right away."

The moment the girl closed the door behind her, Lorna walked over to the bed table, where just two days ago she had placed the ribbon-tied stack of Paul's letters, along with the antique locket that held the miniature. She removed the locket first. Using the tip of her fingernail, she pried loose the delicate gold frame that held the portrait in place, and released the miniature.

The locket had belonged to her mother, so Lorna slipped it around her neck until she could return it to her jewelry box, then she tossed the miniature back into the drawer, where it could remain for eternity for all she cared. That accomplished, she removed the stack of once-treasured letters—letters that had been read so often the paper had become worn from constant folding and unfolding. She paused for a moment, feeling the familiar weight of the ribbon-tied bundle. What joy those letters had brought her—joy, and friendship, and dreams for the future.

Lorna swallowed, hoping to relieve the tightness in her throat. It did not work. "Foolish dreams," she muttered. "Illusions."

Ignoring the hurt, she swallowed again, then she crossed the room to the fireplace, where she bent down and laid the little bundle on the grate. The letters did not ignite instantly as the *Times* had done, but in less than a minute the flames began to nibble at the edges of the writing paper, turning them brown and making them curl. First the bottom letter, then the next, and the next after that.

The smoke from the burning vellum stung Lorna's eyes; at least, that is what she told herself caused the tears that spilled down her cheeks. Finally, when nothing remained of the correspondence but ash, Lorna swiped her sleeve across her damp face, then she walked over to the bed, removed the blue ridding habit, and began preparing herself for the evening ahead.

"And this is Mrs. Phillips," Lady Clement said, indicating a plump, bejeweled lady who stood beside her equally rotund husband, "and Mr. Phillips. Their home is scarce two miles from here, and we have known them for years."

"How do you do, Miss Maitland?"

Lorna curtsied. "Ma'am."

The matron smiled at Lorna before glancing toward the fireplace, where Paul stood, his handsome profile outlined by the light from the silver candelabrum on the mantel. "Such a beautiful young man."

Though no one responded to her comment, the

lady seemed not to notice, and after breathing a sigh, she returned her attention to Lorna. "What a very exciting evening this must be for you, Miss Maitland."

Lorna did not reply; instead, she gave her attention to smoothing out a wrinkle she had just discovered in her lilac kid glove.

Mr. Phillips, a jolly-looking sort, winked at his wife, then whispered an aside to her that was loud enough to be heard by at least half the occupants of the room. "If I know anything of young men," he said, "the evening is likely to become even more exciting, eh, my dear?"

His wife giggled like a schoolroom miss, but Lorna merely curtsied, then turned to introduce Analise to the couple.

Though Lorna would not have guessed it, Analise was proving to be a rock. She had come to Lorna's bedchamber just moments before the first gong sounded and informed her, in no uncertain terms, that she meant for them to go down to the blue drawing room together.

"Your father told me what has happened," she said, "and I know my part."

"Your part?"

"I am to say nothing about you and Lieutenant Clement. No matter who asks, I am to smile prettily and change the subject."

"Did my father tell you to do that?"

Analise shook her head, causing one of her thick, dark curls to dance against her cheek. "Calvin's instructions were that I was to play dumb."

Lorna smothered a laugh. "And can you do that?"

"Oh, yes. Nothing easier, I assure you."

Unconvinced, Lorna had donned her gloves and followed the beauty into the corridor.

Lorna had chosen to wear her lilac sarcenet again.

To wear a dress she had previously worn for a family dinner was Lorna's way of declaring that the evening was no more worthy of distinction than any other. Analise, on the other hand, had dressed as if for a special party, donning a woodbine green creation of tussore silk that hugged her feminine curves and made her appear at least six years younger than her thirty years.

Her hair had been arranged in cascading curls, with a row of pearls entwined among the silken strands, and the effect was quite eye-catching. When the two young ladies entered the drawing room, more than one gentleman stared in awe at the vision in green, and for once, Lorna was thankful for her beautiful relative.

"What think you, lovely creature?" Mr. Phillips asked Analise, "of your cousin's exciting news?"

"Oh, we are not truly cousins," Analise replied. "Though Lorna and her father treat me as quite one of the family, it was my husband and Lorna's mother who were related. Second cousins, once removed, I believe. Or was it twice removed?"

Analise surprised the gentleman by rapping him on the wrist with her fan, then she bestowed upon him a dazzling smile that prompted him to tweak his droopy mustache. "La, sir," she said, "you must not get me started trying to make sense of family trees, for I vow I have not the head for it."

"Excuse us," Lorna said, locking her arm with Analise's, "but we have not yet been introduced to that lady and gentleman across the room."

What Lady Clement thought of such singular behavior, Lorna neither knew nor cared, it was enough that her hostess led them to the next guest, then the next, until they had met the entire party. Each time Lorna would divert any questions by introducing Analise, who took over the conversation.

During the round of introductions, Lorna noticed that Paul remained by the fireplace, looking like a rabbit caught in a snare, while two middle-aged gentlemen clamped him on the shoulder and pumped his hand as if in congratulations.

Lorna overheard more than one matron whisper behind her fan, speculating on the time the formal announcement would be made, but with Analise's help she managed to avoid any direct confrontations.

As for Calvin Maitland, he stood at the far end of the drawing room, enjoying a coze with Stephen Rutledge. At least *he* was enjoying it. The major, on the other hand, appeared much more interested in Lorna's progress around the room.

Earlier Calvin had noticed that the military gentleman was only half listening to him, for he kept looking toward the drawing room door. Then, once Lorna and Analise had finally arrived, the major contributed only the occasional monosyllable to the conversation. He seldom took his eyes off Lorna, and once when she looked their way, the younger man lifted his hand in salute, as if he wished to get her attention.

The signal did not succeed in its objective, for Lady Clement whisked her guest off to meet another of the neighbors.

"The ladies look quite handsome this evening," Calvin said, "even if I do say so myself."

"What?" Stephen looked at him as if he was not certain what had been said.

"Lorna and Analise. They look nice, do you not agree?"

"Oh, yes. Of course."

"You can credit it ter my partiality if you like, Major, but I cannot remember when I have seen two lovelier females. The one dark, the other fair. My daughter is in especially fine looks, wouldn't you say?"

The major looked at him then, his face more serious than Calvin had ever seen it. "Your daughter is as she ever was, sir, the most beautiful woman I have ever met."

If Calvin Maitland found anything remarkable in the younger man's observation, he kept it to himself; instead, he asked Stephen if he intended to remain at Clement Park for very much longer.

"I do not think so, sir."

"Do you return to Derbyshire?

"I do, actually. Just before I left Belgium, I received word that my great-uncle had died. His home was in Derbyshire, and I have been putting off paying a visit to the place."

"My condolences on your loss, lad. Were you and your great-uncle close?"

"Not at all. He disapproved of my father's way of life, and as a result, they never spoke. I do not think I saw the old gentleman above twice in my entire life. I was surprised to discover from the lawyer that I am my great-uncle's nearest relative. Therefore, it falls to me to see to his business affairs."

Their chat was cut short by the arrival of the butler, who announced that dinner was served, and though Stephen moved quickly to see if he might escort Lorna, Paul was there before him. "May I?" Paul asked. The lady gave him a stare cool enough to produce frostbite, but she took his proffered arm just the same and allowed him to escort her to the dining room.

Foiled in his second attempt to claim Lorna's attention, Stephen offered his arm to one of the neighbors, a middle-aged lady with an impressive nose and rather protuberant eyes. He liked her immediately, for she had an acerbic wit, and as it turned out, her place card was next to his.

The long, damask-covered table was set with even more formality than usual, with gold-trimmed charger plates and enough crystal wineglasses to accommodate four different selections. Thankfully, with the addition of the dozen neighbors, conversation flowed as freely as the wine, and as the meal progressed, Stephen discovered that his dinner companion was an old friend of Sir Duncan's.

"He was such a beautiful boy," she said with a sigh. "I quite adored him, and I might have married him if I had been endowed with either a handsomer dowry or a handsomer face."

Stephen found it difficult to maintain a straight face. "The loss, dear lady, was most definitely Sir Duncan's."

"Oh, I quite agree, Major. Now that I am no longer an impressionable girl."

"If I may ask, ma'am, whom did you marry?"

"I chose Harry," she said, motioning toward a gaunt-looking, gray-haired man who sat to Lorna's right. "He is not much to look at, my Harry, but he proved a happy choice, and I would not exchange him for a dozen Adonises."

She leaned closer, lowering her voice. "Especially since Duncan went through his wife's dowry with amazing speed."

Though Stephen did not encourage this line of conversation, neither did he discourage it, and the lady took his silence for interest. "Duncan inherited a great many debts," she said, "and to his credit, he has succeeded in adding substantially to the number. Now the estate is mortgaged to the hilt. Which is, I suppose, the reason for this rather unexpected dinner party. To make it all official."

Stephen mumbled something; he hoped it would

sound as if he were listening. In truth, he had not really heard that last bit, something about the dinner party being unexpected. He could not concentrate on what was ancient gossip, not when he desperately wanted to know if Lorna had read his letter. Under the guise of looking at the husband of his dinner companion, Stephen stared at Lorna, willing her to look at him.

Her full attention was focused on her plate, a most unusual breach of etiquette for a young lady of Lorna Maitland's innate politeness. Furthermore, she was not eating. With fork in hand, she had done nothing more than push a morsel of capered fillet an inch in either direction, without once lifting a bite of food to her mouth. When she finally looked up from her plate, her face wore a fixed expression—an almost masklike serenity—that successfully concealed her thoughts from any chance observer.

For a moment Stephen wondered if she was despondent, or angry with him, or both, as a result of reading his letter. Then she looked across the wide expanse of table, and her gaze locked with his. At first she showed no reaction, then a small, nearly imperceptible smile turned up the corners of her lips.

She had not read the letter! If she had, she would never have favored him with that sweet, friendly smile.

"The neighborhood was abuzz the entire day," the lady beside him continued. "What with the notice in the *Times*, then the sudden arrival of the invitation to dinner to meet the young lady. Of course, we are all obliged to act as if we have no idea what is to be announced this evening. Still—"

"Excuse me?" The lady's words had finally penetrated Stephen's consciousness. "What did you say?"

"Why, only that we will all be required to *ooh* and *ahh*, and act surprised when Sir Duncan and Lady

Clement make the formal announcement of their son's betrothal."

Stephen sat in stunned silence while the lady, totally unaware that her last bit of gossip had riveted the gentleman's attention to her, lifted her wineglass and held it up to the light of the chandelier to examine the color of the liquid. "Everyone is acting very closemouthed," she continued, "but I suppose they must do so until the other guests arrive after dinner."

Her examination of the wine completed, she waved the glass beneath that beak of a nose, then took an exploratory sip of the fruity liquid. She frowned, then without a word, she set the goblet on the table and pushed it some distance from her. "I do hope Sir Duncan has not planned to economize by foisting some inferior champagne upon us when the announcement is finally made. It is so much more romantic, do you not agree, Major? To toast the happy couple with a really fine vintage?"

Stephen did *not* agree. Not at all.

For his part, he did not want to toast the couple with champagne or any other beverage, not unless the wine was laced with some substance that would cause the entire dinner party to fall to the floor in a faint. All except for Lorna, of course. Then he could drag her into some secluded spot and tell her all the things he had written in his letter.

Because there was little chance of some dozen or more guests being so accommodating as to faint, Stephen began to plan some way by which he could waylay Lorna before the time came to make the announcement. She did not love Paul Clement. She could not. And all Stephen needed was a few minutes in which to talk to her.

Throughout the remainder of the dinner, he pretended to listen to the lady beside him, yet all the while he planned his strategy.

After the ladies rose to leave the gentlemen to their port, Stephen remained at the dining table only long enough to allay any suspicions, then he excused himself and left the room. He went immediately to the morning room, the only place he could even hope to have a moment's private conversation, then summoned one of the footmen, slipped the fellow a gold sovereign, and told him to find Miss Maitland and ask her to spare him a moment.

"Be careful that no one else hears you deliver the message."

"I will be the soul of discretion," the fellow assured him.

After pocketing the money, the servant went directly to the blue drawing room, where the ladies had reconvened. Moving as unobtrusively as possible, he slipped past the door, then he found himself a spot in a far corner where he remained until he spied the young lady sitting on a settee, apparently deep in conversation with a beauty in green. A quarter hour had passed before he found an opportunity to deliver the major's message.

Deuce take it! Where is she?
Stephen had no way of knowing the hour, but from the number of times he had paced from one end of the dimly lit room to the other, he knew he had waited an unconscionable time for Lorna to meet him. He had lit a single candle, leaving it where he had found it on the mantelpiece, and though it cast the room in shadows, Stephen could see enough to pace. He had reached the window embrasure for what must be the hundredth time when he heard someone turn the handle of the door.

"In here, miss," the footman said.

Unfortunately, the man had just stepped aside to allow Lorna to enter when someone called her name.

"Miss Maitland?" Paul Clement said. "Is that you?"

"As you see," she replied.

The footman, obviously deeming it prudent to play least in sight, disappeared with all speed, leaving Lorna alone in the doorway.

"I received a message that a gentleman wished to see me," she said. "I assumed it was my father. Was it you, sir?"

"No," Paul replied. "But perhaps it should have been. May we speak privately for a moment?"

The lady said nothing, merely stepped into the room, leaving the door open wide so that Paul could join her. Because Stephen feared his presence might cause a scene that would embarrass her, he stepped within the window embrasure and closed the thick velvet drapery. Not the least concerned about the less than honorable act of eavesdropping, he parted the velvet just enough so he could see what transpired.

Lorna strode across the room to the fireplace, where a single candle burned on the mantelpiece. She did not bother lighting the entire brace, for it occurred to her that this interview might be less awkward if she could not see Paul all that well. Heaven knew, her face was already warm with embarrassment, and she was glad he could not see the red that must be blazing in her cheeks.

When the footman had whispered to Lorna that a gentleman wished to speak with her, she had assumed it was her father, but she had been too happy to quit the drawing room to question the servant too closely. Anything to escape the company of Lady Clement and those women with their smiling, expectant faces. If Lorna had suspected she was to meet Paul, however, she might have remained on the little settee, with her ally, Analise, by her side.

"Well?" she said, turning to stare at the man she

had once thought she loved, "what is it you wish to say to me, Lieutenant? You will forgive me if I appear confused, but you have had the better part of a week to seek me out, and yet you did not do so. Why, then, did you choose tonight, when the house if filled with company?"

Paul crossed the room, stopping scarce three feet away from her. He looked not at Lorna but at the candle flame. "I apologize if my timing is inappropriate, Miss Maitland. Perhaps we should have spoken sooner, but we did not, and what is done is done. Be that as it may, you cannot be unaware of the significance of this party."

"No, sir. I am fully cognizant of its significance. What has me mystified is why you, and your parents, thought I would stand by meekly and allow you to take from me a decision that should have been mine alone to make."

"I see you are overset, Miss Maitland, but surely you must see that my mother has handled everything to a nicety."

"No. I am afraid it see nothing of the sort."

"But—"

"Do you and your family think me so irrelevant that you may, without so much as a by-your-leave, act in a manner that will determine the course of my life?"

"Our lives," Paul corrected. "We are, after all, betrothed."

Lorna stiffened. "Is that a fact?"

"Of course. It is all arranged." He took one step closer, looking at her in the glow of the candlelight. "And now I think about it, it may not be such a bad thing after all. You look quite pretty tonight, prettier than I had expected, and you appear to know how to conduct yourself in public."

If Lorna had not been so furious, she might have

laughed. "Sir, you will turn my head with such sweet talk."

Before Lorna even suspected what he meant to do, Paul reached out and caught her hand, then pulled her into his arms. "Now that our engagement is about to become official," he said, "I find I should like to seal the bargain with a kiss."

·Chapter Twelve

The kiss took Lorna by surprise, and it began and ended before she had time to think what to do. Paul's lips descended on hers, and for some reason she did not protest the intimacy. Perhaps some infinitesimal part of her still recalled the joy his letters had occasioned, and the friendship, the caring that had grown in her heart with each succeeding missive. Whatever the rationale, she let him kiss her.

Actually, she had imagined this kiss a million times; imagined it and longed for it to happen. After all, this was the man whose portrait she had gazed upon numerous times a day for nearly a year, and whose letters she had read and reread until the paper had become worn with handling.

Lorna had been kissed twice before in her life—once by the blacksmith's son when she was newly turned thirteen, and again last December at the Plemstock monthly assembly. On the latter occasion, a gentleman visiting the area had imbibed a bit too much Christmas punch, and in his confusion he had mistaken Lorna for the daughter of his host.

Both those experiences had been fumbling attempts executed ineptly by males who were either too young or too inebriated to exhibit the least finesse. And yet, Lorna preferred either one of those kisses to the feel of Paul Clement's mouth upon hers.

His lips were cold, yet his hands and mouth were

demanding, selfishly so. They sought to be pleased
without displaying the least interest in pleasing.

Even allowing for her inexperience, Lorna knew
instinctively that a kiss should be shared; both parties
should give and receive pleasure. As well, there
ought to be passion mingled with tender regard. And
when the kiss was finished, the lovers should experience a warmth and contentment, and perhaps even
a wish to exchange yet another kiss.

After Paul had kissed her, all Lorna experienced
was disappointment. No warmth. No contentment.
And certainly no wish to repeat the process.

Heartsick with this final disappointment in the
man who had figured in all her dreams, Lorna
prayed he would not try to kiss her again, for she
did not wish to be obliged to scream for help. Tomorrow would bring enough gossip down upon her, she
did not need the ignominy of being caught fighting
off unwanted advances.

Thankfully, Paul seemed content with the one kiss,
for he let her go and stepped back. As Lorna looked
up at him, she saw upon his chiseled face a self-
satisfied smirk—a look that said, more clearly than
words, that he believed he had been challenged and
had come through the contest the victor.

At that smug look, Lorna's insides roiled and
threatened to cast up the few sips of wine she had
drunk at dinner. She wanted to wipe her gloved
hand across her mouth to remove the trace of his
lips, and yet she did not. Something stayed her hand;
she supposed it was the emptiness she felt as she
laid to rest the last vestige of doubt that she might
still love Paul Clement.

"Shall we go up to the drawing room?" he asked.
"Our guests are waiting."

His confident manner implied that he fully expected her to comply with his wishes, but when he

offered her his arm, Lorna did not take it. "You go on ahead. I need a moment to myself."

Paul must have assumed that her need for privacy was a compliment to his romantic expertise, for he gave her a knowing smile. "You take all the time you need, my dear." He straightened his neckcloth, then adjusted his coat. "Perhaps it would be as well if we were not seen entering the room together. Not tonight, at least. As for tomorrow . . ."

He let the comment go uncompleted, then he walked to the door, which was still ajar. Before he exited the room, he turned to look at her, though he could not have seen more than the outline of her face in the dim light. "Do not delay overlong," he said. "I hear more guests arriving, and my father wishes to make the announcement as soon as possible."

When the door finally clicked shut behind Paul, Lorna took a deep breath and exhaled loudly.

"So, madam," said a voice from the far side of the room, "his kisses left you sighing for more."

Lorna turned quickly, staring toward the window. The drapery had been thrown wide, and the moonlight coming through the glass panes revealed a tall, broad-shouldered man standing in the embrasure. Not that she needed light to tell her who had spoken.

"Stephen! How long have you been there?"

"Long enough."

"You should have let your presence be known."

"What? And miss that tender scene?"

For some reason Lorna did not wish to examine, his mocking words caused an empty feeling deep within her chest. "It was not . . . he just . . ." She drew another deep breath. "You do not understand."

"I understand perfectly, madam. Apparently, the prospect of being the future Lady Clement was more appealing to you than I had thought. Especially if after all you have seen and heard, you still mean to marry that selfish bastard."

Lorna gasped. "How dare you speak to me in that manner! My motives and my actions are no concern of yours."

He covered the distance between them in five angry strides. "And what if I make them my concern?"

Before she could answer, Stephen caught her by the shoulders and pulled her to within inches of his face. "Did his kiss prove nothing to you?"

"You watched him kiss me? How . . . how despicable!"

Stephen's powerful fingers dug into the soft flesh of her shoulders. "You find *my* actions despicable? What of yours? You allowed yourself to be kissed by that fortune hunting . . ."

Words seemed to fail him, and he yanked her against his chest. "Deuce take it, Lorna, you cannot have enjoyed that kiss."

Lorna wanted to protest this ungentlemanly treatment, but from the moment Stephen had touched her, her lungs had played her false, leaving her almost too breathless to speak. Now, with her breasts pressed against his hard chest, her heart had begun to beat so painfully she thought she might faint.

And yet, she did not faint. Instead, she caught the lapels of his coat, clinging to them for support. Uncertain what to think of Stephen's anger, Lorna tilted her head back so she could look into his eyes. This close, they reminded her of a midnight sky, deep and dark, yet lit by some distant star.

While she gazed at him, trying to discern the meaning of that light, he slipped his right arm around her waist, drawing the full length of her against his body. When she did not protest, he slid his left hand up her shoulder and around to the back of her neck. The slow, deliberate movement sent shafts of awareness all the way to her toes, and when his fingers splayed and became entangled in her hair, Lorna nestled her head in his palm.

"Stephen, you—"

"Shhh. If you are being so free with your kisses," his whispered, his voice disturbingly husky, "I think it only fair that you let me show you what a real kiss can be."

He said no more, simply lowered his face to hers and claimed her lips. At first the contact was soft, his firm lips tasting, testing hers. Then, when Lorna thought nothing could be more wonderful than the sensations that warmed every inch of her skin, Stephen tightened his arms around her, molding her willing body to his. As he deepened the kiss, the warmth became a fire that threatened to turn her to ashes.

Lorna released his lapels and slipped her arms around his waist, willing the kiss to go on forever. She had never felt anything as thrilling as Stephen's strong arms holding her close, and nothing as magical as his mouth upon hers, coaxing her to respond, giving her untold pleasure while taking what she freely gave.

Her body had gone limp, and when Stephen finally lifted his head, Lorna found that her legs would not sustain her weight. She would have fallen if he had not kept his arm around her waist. "Stephen," she murmured, "I never knew a kiss could be so—"

"Lorna?" A soft tap sounded at the door. "Lorna? It is Analise. Are you there?"

When the knob began to turn, Lorna wriggled out of Stephen's arms and hurried to the door to intercept the intruder. She did not want Analise to see her alone with Stephen in a darkened room. She knew her relative; possessed of more hair than wit,

the widow might misunderstand and assume that
they . . . that Lorna and Stephen had . . . Had what?

Lorna did not want to put a name to what had
happened between her and Stephen Rutledge. Not
yet. Not before she had some privacy in which to
ponder the significance of that kiss and her response
to it. Now was not the time to be plagued with all
sorts of questions from her relative—questions for
which Lorna had no answers.

"I am coming, Analise. Wait there."

Though Lorna would have liked nothing better
than to continue up the stairs to her bedchamber, she
knew there was no escaping the scene that awaited
her in the blue drawing room. With no recourse but
to face the inevitable, she slipped her arm through
Analise's, and the two women walked down the long
corridor toward the waiting guests.

As they neared the drawing room, Lorna heard
music. Someone was playing the pianoforte, per-
forming a beautiful and evocative melody by Scar-
latti. When a footman opened the door for them,
Lorna was surprised—no, shocked—to see Paul sitting at the instrument, his fingers gliding across the
ivory keys with a deftness that would have pleased
the Italian composer.

The song ended just moments after they arrived,
and the two dozen or so guests applauded with sincere appreciation of Paul's talent.

"Bravo!" one man shouted.

"So talented," a lady remarked.

"He was always gifted," another replied. "Even as
a child, he played like an angel."

Even Analise applauded. "I did not know the lieutenant played the piano."

"Nor I," Lorna said.

Even as the words left her lips, she recalled the

letter in which Paul had said that *her* lack of musical skill could never match *his* lack of musical discernment. Why had he chosen to lie to her? She could understand a person being modest enough not to admit to being a virtuoso, but Paul had gone so far as to say he had a tin ear, when nothing could have been further from the truth. Paul's touch, his timing, his artistry were impeccable.

As Lorna puzzled over his possible motive for telling her that he was "As near to being tone deaf as made no difference," one of the guests spoke to her, interrupting her thoughts.

"What of you, Miss Maitland? Will you favor us with a selection?"

Lorna shook her head. "I neither play nor sing, sir, so I beg you will excuse me."

"Then what about you?" asked the self-appointed master of ceremonies.

At first Lorna thought he spoke to Analise, but she soon realized that his gaze was directed at someone who stood just behind her.

"Are you musical?" he asked.

"Not at all," Stephen replied.

"Come, come," the gentleman protested. "I know you military types. It never fails, let two soldiers meet near a pianoforte, and a rousing tune cannot be far behind. What say you, Major? Do not be shy."

"In this instance, sir, shyness has nothing to do with it. The sad truth is that I am quite tone deaf. Mine is a tin ear."

The gentleman laughed. "In that case, Major, I suppose we shall have to look elsewhere for further entertainment."

Someone else was asked to favor them with a song, but Lorna never knew who that person was, nor did she hear their reply. She heard nothing but the echo inside her head. The words "tin ear, tin ear" sounded so loudly they overpowered everything else, and as the echo went on and on, Lorna began to shiver.

Stephen has a tin ear, while Paul plays the pianoforte like an angel.

Hard upon that thought came a memory that had puzzled Lorna from the first moment she met Stephen. He had been on horseback, and as the Maitland's coach crunched over the gravel of the Clement Park carriageway, Stephen had ridden up beside them, greeting Thomas and tipping his hat to Lorna.

"Good day, ma'am," he had said. "If you are Miss Lorna Maitland, allow me to tell you how pleased I am to make your acquaintance at last."

Before that moment, Lorna had not known of Stephen Rutledge's existence, yet he had chuckled and said he was glad to meet her at last.

Stephen always laughed. His was such a sunny disposition, while Paul's had proved so reserved it seemed almost morose. From the beginning, Lorna had felt distanced from Paul. At the same time, Stephen had been so amiable she had felt compelled to discourage his friendly overtures. Of course, she had finally given in to those overtures—given in with an ease that was not her usual manner.

Because her father's wealth attracted fortune hunters, Lorna had learned to be wary of young gentlemen, and her initial response to them was always guarded. Yet she had soon found herself conversing with Stephen in a relaxed manner, as though they were old friends. Friends who could say whatever they wished to one another, without fear of—

No! Lorna breathed deeply in an attempt to calm the suspicion that had taken root. It was preposterous. How could she even think such a thing? In the confusion of this interminable evening, she was allowing her imagination to play her false.

Lorna's head began to ache with the disorder of

her thoughts. She would not—could not—believe that anyone would play such a cruel hoax upon her. Especially not Stephen. Yet it would explain so much—Paul's coolness when she had expected warmth; his treating her like a stranger when she had thought they were friends.

Lorna reeled from the suspicion that took hold of her and would not let go. She must have squeezed Analise's arm, for the beauty gasped.

"Lorna?" she asked. "Are you ill? Your face is ghostly white. Shall I find you a place to sit?"

Ignoring Analise's offer, Lorna turned slowly, unable to stop herself, and looked up at Stephen. She wanted to hear him deny everything. She wanted him to tell her that he had not been making a May game of her for nearly a year.

The question she needed to ask stuck in her throat, very nearly choking her, and all she could say was, "The letters."

He must have read her anguish in her eyes, for he reached out and took her hand. "Forgive me, my friend. I never meant—"

"Was it one of your jests?"

Lorna could no longer look at him, so she stared at his hand holding hers. The sight caused an ache that began in her midsection and moved up to her chest, lodging painfully in her heart. The warmth of his skin mocked her. The strength of his fingers holding hers was an indictment of her gullibility. Feeling like the biggest fool in nature, Lorna eased her hand from his and stepped back.

"Please," he said, "let me explain."

She turned away, pretending not to hear him. Instead, she leaned toward Analise. "I do feel unwell," she said, "and I must have some air. Will you find Papa and tell him that I . . ." The words died in her throat.

"Tell him what?" Analise asked.

Lorna did not reply; she could not, for the piano performance had ended, and during the polite applause that followed, Paul's father had stepped to the front of the room, a champagne glass in his hand.

At the sight of that innocent-looking crystal, Lorna knew she had delayed too long. There was no escaping now. As if wrapped in some sort of emotional shroud, she stood unmoving, incapable of speech or thought. Overcome by the sense of impending doom, she could only stare.

Sir Duncan smiled, very much the affable host. "Please," he said, "may I have everyone's attention?"

Naturally, all eyes turned to him. An expectant hush filled the room.

"Friends," he said, "Lady Clement and I hope you are enjoying the evening, and we wish to thank you for coming to us on such short notice." He looked around the room, inclining his head toward one or two of the ladies. "From the amount of discreet whispering that has been going on behind lace fans, it would appear that some of you suspect there is more to the invitation than my desire to look upon your lovely faces."

The guests laughed in appreciation of their host's humor. Once the laughter had subsided, Sir Duncan continued. "I shall not keep you guessing for very much longer. Instead, I call your attention to the presence of the servants, who will pass among you with trays bearing glasses of champagne. I ask you all to join me in a toast."

He said nothing more until each of the guests had received their champagne. When the soft murmurs of their voices faded, and each person turned again toward their host, Sir Duncan raised his glass. "My friends," he said, "I would like to announce—"

"A moment, there," Calvin Maitland said. "Before

you continue, Sir Duncan, I have a few words ter say."

Like everyone else, Lorna turned to stare at her father. Several dozen voices buzzed their surprise at the interruption, but Sir Duncan silenced them with a wave of his hand. Though his smile now appeared forced, he inclined his head toward Lorna's father. "Yes, Mr. Maitland? You wished to speak?"

"I did, indeed, sir. First, allow me ter thank you and Lady Clement for this excellent party. No young lady could ask for better. Still, if there are announcements ter be made, I think it more fitting that I, the young lady's father, make them."

"By all means," Sir Duncan said. His face looked decidedly pasty, but his voice still held a note of hope. "I bow to your right as the father of the br—"

"If you please," Calvin Maitland interrupted, "lift your glasses, one and all, in toast ter the happy couple." He turned toward Lorna, his glass held high. "Happiness and all prosperity ter my daughter, Miss Lorna Maitland, and ter her fiancé, Major Stephen Rutledge."

Chapter Thirteen

The buzz in the room was nothing compared to the clamor going on inside Lorna's head. Had her father gone mad, or had she? Had he really named Stephen Rutledge as her fiancé?

Apparently *she* had lost all touch with reality, for Stephen stepped beside her and placed his hand at the back of her waist. Then, while all around them people stared, their glasses halfway to their mouths, Stephen took a sip of his champagne, then held his glass to Lorna's lips. "Drink," he whispered.

The single word may have been softly spoken, but there was steel behind it. It was an order, and still bemused, Lorna obeyed. She felt the cool liquid moisten her lips, then an infinitesimal amount of wine touched her tongue. She swallowed.

"And now," Stephen said, still in that military, I-will-be-obeyed voice, "Analise will take you to your room."

"But—"

"Now!" he said.

If haste was anything to go by, Analise was eager to flee the commotion caused by Calvin's announcement, for she caught Lorna by the arm and more or less dragged her from the drawing room. Once the door was closed behind them, she continued to pull Lorna toward the stairs that gave access to the next level and the guests' bedchambers.

As for the young lady with the two fiancés, she allowed herself to be led, but when she was halfway up the stairs she began to tremble and was obliged to grasp the ornately carved banister to keep from falling. "I think I may be losing my sanity," she said, "for I do not know what just happened in there."

"Your father happened," the lady in green replied, staring at her relative in surprise. "You should have known that Calvin would make things right. He always does."

The tall case clock outside Stephen's bedchamber door chimed six times, and while the final tone echoed down the quiet corridor, Stephen folded the note he had just written and affixed a plain green wafer. After glancing toward the window, where the still-dark sky showed faint traces of dawn's pink light, he turned back to the desk and wrote Thomas's name across the front of the folded vellum.

Stephen had already changed into his traveling clothes, and his portmanteau stood by the bed, packed, strapped, and ready to be taken belowstairs. He would not leave Clement Park, however, without first apologizing to Thomas for canceling the promised fishing trip.

He did not wish to leave so fresh upon the heels of last night's disastrous party; in fact, he would have preferred to stay and face the day and Paul Clement. Unfortunately, Calvin Maitland had not agreed with Stephen, and at some point during the half-hour argument between the two men—the argument that followed the larger and louder shouting match between Lorna's father and the Clement family—the wiser head had prevailed. Mr. Maitland had convinced Stephen that it would be better for all concerned if he left the premises straightaway.

"You're a brave lad, no one would dispute that

fact, but I've no wish ter see you challenged ter a duel. The legalities of a broken engagement I can handle, but I'd no be able ter live with myself if you were injured as a result of this sorry business. The blame is, after all, mine and mine alone."

Stephen shook his head. "No, sir. I cannot let you take full credit for this fiasco. It was I who wrote the letters. Without them, none of this would have happened."

"We'll never know that for certain, Major. But no matter where the truth lies, I'll give you my hand in friendship and thank you for your prompt action before the guests. There'll be gossip for sure, and speculation enough ter keep the tabbies talking till Michaelmas, but I think we managed to avoid a real scandal. As for Sir Duncan and his lady, they have promised ter go along with the story that the announcement in the *Times* was a misprint."

"Most generous of them," Stephen said, his voice filled with sarcasm. "Care to tell me how much that little concession cost you?"

"I do not, you impudent dog."

Shortly afterward, the men had shaken each other's hand, then said their good-byes. Now, Stephen had only to deliver the note to Thomas, then he could leave Clement Park for good.

With that thought in mind, he climbed the narrow, utilitarian stairs that led to the third-floor nursery, walking softly so as not to awaken anyone. He did not knock upon the door, but opened it quietly and looked toward the single cot where Thomas slept. The boy looked surprisingly small and fragile lying there on his side, with his knees drawn up and his hands tucked beneath his freckled face. His wheat gold hair—so like Lorna's—was mussed, and at some time during the night he had thrown off the bedcovers, leaving nothing but his coarse linen nightshirt to ward off the chilly air.

If the room had boasted a fire earlier, it had long since died out, so after Stephen set the note on the bedside table, where the boy would see it when he awoke, he drew the cover up over the lad's shoulders and whispered his farewell. He had reached the door when Thomas spoke his name.

"Is that you, Major Rutledge? Is it time to get up? Have I overslept?" Thomas threw back the covers and sat up, his thin legs dangling over the side of the bed. "Just give me two minutes, sir, and I will be ready to go."

"Stay, lad. I am afraid our fishing expedition will have to be postponed, for I must leave right away." He pointed to the bedside table. "I left you a note explaining the whole."

Thomas rubbed his knuckles across his sleep-heavy eyelids, but he did not reach for the note. "I . . . I shall read it later," he said.

Stephen heard the disappointment in the boy's voice, and he knew he could not leave like this. Never mind who objected to his telling the story, this child had no part in the arguments of the adults, and he deserved something more than a note and a hasty good-bye.

"You will find out soon enough," Stephen said, "that your cousin Lorna is no longer engaged to marry Lieutenant Clement. The betrothal was ended last evening, with harsh words spoken on both sides. For that reason I feel certain that those of you from Epping Grange will be returning there as soon as arrangements can be made."

"My mother and I do not live at the Grange." As if to avoid making eye contact, Thomas stuck his finger through a small hole he discovered in the sleeve of his nightshirt. "I wish the Grange was our home, but it is not. We have lodgings in Tunbridge Wells."

Some guarded quality in the boy's voice told Stephen that he did not wish to return to the famous spa town. "Is there something about Tunbridge Wells that you do not like?"

When Thomas did not answer, Stephen rephrased the question. "Perhaps that which you dislike is not some *thing* but some *one*."

So much had happened since yesterday that Stephen had forgotten about the man Thomas thought he saw in the stables of the Talbot Inn. "Is it the man who frightened you yesterday? The one with red hair? What was his name again, Treherne?"

When the boy nodded, Stephen walked over and sat on the edge of the cot. "Who is this man? And what does he have to do with you?"

"He wants to marry my mother."

"I see." Stephen was inclined to think this a case of a child not wanting to share his mother, but the boy disabused him of that notion.

"Mother does not wish to marry him."

"Are you certain? Children do not always understand what adults need and want. Perhaps your mother is lonely. I daresay you will be going off to school soon. Do you not think she would be happier, once you are no longer with her every day, if she had someone to keep her company?"

"Oh, yes, I know she would be happier, and if she had a husband, she would not have to worry so about the tradesmen's bills. But she does not wish to marry Felix Treherne. Or anyone else."

"Are you quite certain?"

"Oh, yes, sir."

Stephen was surprised, not that she did not wish to marry this Treherne fellow, but that she was content to remain single. Analise Whidby was a beautiful young woman, and she must have dozens of suitors, most of whom would be quite happy to assume the burden of paying the tradesmen's bills.

"There is someone *I* wish she would marry."

"If I may ask, Thomas, whom do you wish your mother would marry?"

"Cousin Calvin."

"What!"

Stephen knew that Thomas was devoted to Lorna and to her father, but a marriage between the beautiful Analise, and the blustering wool merchant? The idea positively boggled the mind.

"If she married Cousin Calvin, I could remain at Epping Grange forever. Just me, Mama, Cousin Calvin, and Cousin Lorna."

As Stephen had predicted, the foursome left for Epping Grange just before noon, and when the Maitland chaise and pair rolled down the gravel carriageway toward the wrought iron gates, the three members of the Clement family were conspicuous in their absence. As well, none of the household came to wave their goodbyes. Only Bess, the young maid who had attended Lorna, expressed any sorrow at the unexpected departure.

"Oh, miss," she said, "I'm that sorry about the party and all. If I do say so as shouldn't, what this family needs is someone like you to warm them up a bit. A real breath of spring, you are. And pretty behaved as well, if you'll forgive my saying so."

"Thank you, Bess. Your cheerful manner is the one thing about Clement Park that I will remember with fondness."

The maid began to weep, and when she shook her head, refusing the generous vail Lorna tried to press into her hand, Lorna hugged her and slipped the five-pound note into the girl's apron pocket.

Ten minutes later the Maitland carriage exited the Park and rattled onto the lane that led to the village of Beddingford, less than five miles away. Just before the coachman drove through the village, he reined in the horses long enough to yell to the passengers, asking if anyone wished to stop at the inn for a short rest.

"Drive on," Calvin Maitland shouted. "We none of us wish ter remain in Warwickshire a minute longer than need be."

To Lorna's everlasting gratitude, her father and Analise had little to say during the drive, and if Thomas longed for the constant chatter that had enlivened their journey into Warwickshire, he kept his wishes to himself. What few conversational gambits were tossed into the silence were greeted with monosyllabic replies, and soon each of the four travelers occupied their time by looking out their respective windows.

Actually, though Lorna stared fixedly at the passing landscape, she saw little of the beautiful countryside. As the horses sped through the English heartland, the lovely trees, the picturesque cottages, even the farms with their red earth were little more than a blur, for Lorna's thoughts were occupied to the exclusion of all else.

So much had happened last night, so much that she needed to consider, but upon one topic she would not let herself dwell. She refused to recall those moments in the dimly lit morning room—those moments when Stephen had held her in his arms and kissed her, introducing her to the passion, the fire, the promise of ecstasy a man and a woman could ignite in one another. Any time those traitorous thoughts tried to claim her attention, Lorna banished them immediately with the recollection of Stephen's deception, the cruel hoax he and Paul Clement had played on her.

Her face burned with the recollection of their conspiracy. Why they did it, she still did not know. She did not want to know. It was enough that between them, the two men had broken her heart.

Last night, as she stood in the blue drawing room, her senses had been sent reeling when she realized that she had loved one man on Monday, and loved an entirely different man five days later. Such a drastic change of heart was enough to make any woman question her ability to discern true love. Worse was yet to come, however, for scarce ten minutes later her entire confidence in her intelligence was undermined by the discovery that neither man was who or what she believed him to be.

Liars, both of them.

How they must have laughed at her. All those months when she had opened her heart to one man, she had, in fact, been corresponding to a stranger—someone whose name she did not even know.

Her eyes burned with tears, but Lorna refused to blink and let them fall. She had wept enough tears last night. In truth, she had not known a person could cry for so many hours without ceasing. The combination of anger, hurt, and disillusionment had fed the salty flow, and by the time traces of dawn showed in the sky, Lorna's throat ached and her head pounded as though a miniature pugilist were inside her skull attempting to punch his way out.

While she lay upon her bed, sleep still eluding her, she thought she heard a horse and carriage outside on the gravel, but she had neither enough energy nor sufficient curiosity to go to the window and see who was abroad at such an early hour.

Thomas cleared his throat, as if hesitant to interrupt the silence, and Lorna's attention was brought back to the present. "The major came to tell me good-bye," he said.

"Did he now?" Being gentlemen, the two males occupied the backward-facing seat, so Calvin was obliged to turn his head to look at the youngster beside him. "When was that, my boy?"

"Early this morning, I think. It was still dark, so after he left I went back to sleep."

"A wise move, lad. I wish I had slept more myself."

Lorna wanted to hear nothing of Stephen Rutledge, but short of putting her fingers in her ears, she could not avoid listening to Thomas's remarks.

"He told me he had to return to Derbyshire on important business."

Calvin made a *hmm* noise. "The major said that, did he?"

Thomas shook his head. "He did not actually *say* it. He wrote it in the note he left me."

A note? Lorna made a *humph* noise in her throat, but to her relief, no one seemed to notice. The man had taken leave of his senses to commit himself to paper again. Surely he had written enough letters for one lifetime. After all, he—

No! Lorna bit back a moan. *The letter on the dressing table!*

Lorna had forgotten about the thick missive the footman had brought to her bedchamber yesterday. At the time she had thought Paul had written it, so when she went down to the party, she had left the letter unread. She had not thought of it again until that moment, and for the life of her, she could not recall if it had still been on the dressing table this morning.

Not that she wanted to read it now. She had no interest in anything Stephen Rutledge had to say. Her only concern was that someone else might find those pages and think it was their right to read them. How mortifying if Lady Clement should be that someone, and she should discover what a fool Lorna had been.

Or what if the missive came into the hands of that butler who thought himself too good to wait upon the Maitlands? What if he read it, then shared the contents with the staff in the servants' hall? Or worse yet, what if Bess found the letter?

The maid would never give those pages to someone else, but neither would she destroy them. Lorna groaned, for she knew exactly what Bess would do. The maid would write Lorna's name and direction on the outer page, then she would use part of her five-pound note to post Stephen's letter to Epping Grange.

Chapter Fourteen

Every day Lorna watched for the post. Through what remained of the month of May, then all of June and July, she watched. The letter never came.

During those unseasonably cool summer months, each time one of the grooms rode to the village to collect the newspapers and the post, Lorna found a reason to be at home when the servant returned. Of course, she always gave herself some excuse for her actions, and if anyone happened to see her in the vestibule, standing beside the rosewood console table, where the butler invariably placed the post, she would explain that she was hoping to hear from an old school chum.

To Lorna's everlasting gratitude, no one ever asked her *which* school chum.

The entire household had watched with interest the year-long correspondence between Lorna and Lieutenant Clement, and if their smiles and winks were anything to go by, their anticipation of each letter had matched that of the recipient. Naturally, the more romantic of the servants had been disappointed to discover that the couple, upon meeting face-to-face, had decided they did not suit. Now it appeared they were showing their sympathy for Lorna by allowing her to receive her letters in private.

When August arrived, and Stephen's missive still

had not come, Lorna finally gave up the notion of ever seeing it again. As if to demonstrate the fickleness of life, the next day she found the letter. Or rather, her maid found it, pinned in the bodice of Lorna's blue riding habit.

Oxfordshire had been graced with more than its share of inclement weather that summer, and that particular morning promised to be crisp, yet sunny, a perfect day to ride to Plemstock. Two weeks earlier Lorna had turned over a skep of bees to one of the cottagers, and she always made at least one visit to a new recipient's home, just to assure herself that the bees were adjusting to the move from the Epping Grange apiary.

Thinking she might stop in at the vicarage for a coze with her friend, Anne, Lorna asked her maid to give her green habit a good brushing.

"I'm that sorry, Miss Lorna, but the green wants mending. A right mess you made of it t'other day, for the hem has a tear in it fully eight inches wide."

"Oh, dear. I must have caught my heel in it."

"Most likely you did. Any rood," said the maid, in the familiar manner of one who has been with the family for twenty-plus years. "I've not found a moment to put needle to tread, so you'll have to make do with the old blue habit this time."

Lorna's face must have shown her reluctance, for the plump-cheeked servant said, "I know you've given up wearing the blue, but 'tis not too outdated, I'm thinking, for the likes of Jim Stoddard and his bees."

Actually, its being outdated had nothing to do with Lorna's reason for relegating that particular article of clothing to the back of the chiffonnier. She had not worn the blue habit since her return to Epping Grange, for she did not wish to remember the day she rode to Stratford-upon-Avon with Stephen Rutledge. Most definitely she did not wish to recall that she had worn the blue on that occasion simply because the shade was known as gentian, and Stephen had once likened her eyes to that blue flower.

Knowing she had either to wear the older habit or give up the idea of riding to the village that day, Lorna favored expediency and abandoned her wish for a selective memory. After calling herself a fool for fretting over something that happened almost three months ago, she sighed, then asked Kate to see if she could find the blue.

"I've got it here," the maid said, removing the riding costume from the chiffonnier. "Just let me give it a bit of a look to see if it wants a brushing, then I'll . . . Saints preserve us, what is this?"

"Do not tell me that hem is torn as well."

"No. It's the bodice. There's something pinned inside it. Something right bulky."

"There was nothing there when I wore it last."

"That's as may be, but there's something there now."

Kate put her hand inside the bodice and withdrew a straight pin, which she placed between her lips for safe keeping. When she reached inside the bodice the second time, she withdrew several sheets of vellum.

Lorna gasped. The sheets were folded and sealed with a wafer, and she did not need to see the handwriting to know it was the letter Stephen had written to her the evening of the ill-fated engagement party.

Bess, the young maid from Clement Park, must have pinned the pages into the bodice for safekeeping when she packed Lorna's trunk. That explained why Lorna had not received anything by post.

Kate must have heard the gasp, for she stared at Lorna, speculation in her eyes. Then, as if sensing the importance of the papers, she held them up to the light and examined the handwriting, even though she could not read. "What shall I do with it?" she asked, curiosity in her look and her voice.

Give it to me immediately!

The day of the party, Lorna had left the letter on the dressing table, but this time she would not ignore it. Time had passed—eleven weeks, three days, and ten hours, to be exact—and though she still felt a void deep inside her heart each time she recalled Stephen's perfidy, anger no longer surged through her.

Nothing could excuse what he had done; nonetheless, Lorna wanted very much to know what he had written

Trying for a nonchalant air, she said, "It cannot be so very important, not if it has waited this long. Probably just some tradesman's bill. Toss it on the bed. I will see to it later."

Kate did as she was bid. After she placed the folded pages onto the pink-and-white counterpane, she went about the business of brushing the habit, all else forgotten. Unfortunately, Lorna was not able to summon a similar detachment, for while she dressed and put up her hair, her gaze went constantly to the missive on the bed. With each new glimpse of the vellum, the knot in her stomach pulled just a little bit tighter.

Leave me, Kate! Go!

To Lorna's disappointment, the maid did not heed the unspoken order. Instead, she fetched the skirt of the green habit and her sewing box and took them to the slipper chair by the front window.

"Since you'll be leaving soon, Miss Lorna, I'll just sit here where the light is good and do this mending." Before Lorna could protest, Kate had bitten off a length of thread, wished her mistress an enjoyable ride, and begun to thread her needle.

Not wishing to raise the maid's suspicions, Lorna

did not protest or ask for privacy. Instead, she strolled to the bed, casually picked up the letter, and slipped it inside the bodice where it had resided since May. After drawing on her leather riding gloves, she bid Kate good-bye and exited the bedchamber.

On the whole of the Epping Grange estate there was but one spot where Lorna could be assured of complete privacy, and that place was among the bees. After passing through the front entrance with its handsome oak doors, Lorna stepped onto the rose-bordered carriageway and asked the groom to walk the pretty bay mare for a few minutes.

"I wish to check on the bees."

The groom pulled his forelock, gave a gentle tug to the mare's rein, then walked the animal and his own mount toward the brick columns at the end of the carriageway.

Lorna took the fieldstone footpath, and once she was out of sight of the groom, and anyone who might be watching from one of the windows of the handsome brick and flint house, she hurried down to the stables. From there she ran the next quarter mile to the apiary.

Five skeps remained in her possession, and from each of the tall, domed, twisted-straw hives came a soft, comforting hum. For safety's sake, Lorna was careful not to sit too close to any one skep. When the bees left the hive each day in search of nectar, they flew a circuitous route, but after they had found the nectar, and their little bodies were filled, they returned to the skep by the shortest route possible, the beeline. A wise person did not want to stand in that beeline.

Unmindful of her skirt, Lorna sat upon the ground and rested her back against the deeply furrowed bark of a walnut tree that was at least two hundred years old. Hoping the stately tree would lend her some of its calm, she reached her hand inside her bodice and removed Stephen's letter.

Lorna took a full minute to study the writing on the outer page. She had seen that same handwriting many times over the past year, but this time was different. This time she knew the true identity of the writer. This time she knew the letter came from Stephen Rutledge, and just knowing that he had touched the pages made her hands tremble so badly she had difficulty breaking the wafer and unfolding the vellum.

She had read at least a dozen of Stephen's letters, believing them to be from Paul, and yet even before she read this one, it set her heart racing as none had before it. As she pondered this phenomenon, she realized that the handsome face in the miniature—Paul's face—had never truly matched the picture her mind created as she read the warm, wonderful letters. Now she knew why, for she had only to see her name written on the page to summon Stephen's rugged features, to bring to mind his dark eyes, to recall his smiling mouth.

Stephen's mouth. At the thought, Lorna closed her eyes, remembering the way Stephen had smiled at her, the way he had teased her, and the way he had kissed her. That thrilling, bone-melting kiss had told her so much. It told her that she was more than just the daughter of a wealthy man, that she was, in fact, a desirable woman—a woman who had found the one man in the world who could make her dreams come true.

"Oh, Stephen," she whispered, "why did you make me love you?"

Since no answer was forthcoming, Lorna opened her eyes and began to read.

My dear friend,

There is no good way to begin this letter. What I must tell you will hurt you deeply, and giving you pain is the last thing in the world I wish to do. Furthermore, what I must tell you may cause you to hate me, and if it is any consolation to you, knowing that you hate me will hurt me more than you can possibly know.

Be that as it may, I cannot allow you to marry Paul Clement without first telling you that it was I, and not Paul, who wrote to you from Belgium. Every letter came from my hand. What I did was dishonorable, and I make no excuses for my behavior. Once I had begun to write to you, however, I had not the courage to stop.

Without your letters, I believe I would not have lived through those terrible days during and after Waterloo. Your words kept me sane. Your gentleness, your humanity were all I had to remind me that there was still beauty and goodness in the world.

I held to your letters like a drowning man clutches the hand of his rescuer. That is what you were to me: My rescuer, my lodestar, my angel, my friend.

During the dark days that seemed to go on forever, it was you, and you alone, who made me remember the light.

If, after knowing of my deception, you decide after all to marry Paul, I wish you all the happiness in the world. For myself, I wish three things. Of the first wish I will say nothing, but the second and third wishes are simply that you will one day forgive me for my part in the deception, and that you will never forget that as long as I am upon this earth, I am yours to command.

Your friend,
Stephen Rutledge

Lorna read the pages through twice more, then she folded them and returned them to her bodice. This time, however, she positioned the letter slightly higher than before, so that it was pressed firmly against her heart.

During the ride into Plemstock, Lorna thought of nothing else but Stephen's words. Of course she forgave him. How could she not? When he wrote her all those letters, he was a soldier, alone in the world, and that world was involved in a terrible war. All around him death and destruction reigned, and he took comfort where he found it, in her letters.

As for Paul Clement, after having met him and his family, Lorna did not need special insight to guess why *he* had allowed someone else to write letters to his fiancée. Though Lorna found it lowering to admit that Paul wanted only one thing from her—her dowry—the truth could not be denied. His arrogant belief in his own superiority allowed him to agree to marry Lorna for her money, while thinking her beneath him in every way. No doubt he felt it was too much of a *bother* to write to her.

How it transpired that Stephen began the correspondence, Lorna neither knew nor cared. What mattered was that she fell in love with the man in the letters, and later she fell in love with Stephen Rutledge. Until the night of the party, she had not suspected that the two men were one and the same.

Not that it mattered in the grand scheme of things, for Stephen had left Clement Park the morning after the party. He had done what he meant to do—he had prevented Lorna from marrying a man who was incapable of loving her—then he had gone away, without so much as a word of farewell to her.

Oddly enough, Stephen had succeeded in his mission not by his confession—which Lorna had not read—but by his actions. In everything he did, he unwittingly exposed Paul's cold indifference toward her and her family. Stephen had been unerringly respectful to her father and unfailingly considerate toward Thomas, when everyone else in the house begrudged them the least civility. As well, Stephen had endeared himself to all three of them with his teasing ways and his happy, joyous manners.

Finally, when he kissed her, he proved to Lorna beyond any shadow of doubt that she could never marry Paul. With one kiss, Stephen gave her a glimpse of the passion that should ignite naturally between a man and a woman—the kind of passion whose foundation was an existing bond of respect and affection. After experiencing his tender kiss and the feel of his arms wrapped around her, holding her close, Lorna knew that she wanted nothing less than real love.

She did not regret ending her betrothal to Paul Clement, but now that she knew it was Stephen she loved—had loved all the time—she was forced to face the daunting realization that she would never marry, never have a family of her own. She loved Stephen Rutledge with all her heart and with all her soul, and she would love him for eternity. Unfortunately, he felt only friendship for her.

Though her heart felt as if someone had removed it from her chest and left it exposed to the unforgiving elements, Lorna did not regret loving Stephen. Even if it were possible, she would not change the way she felt about him. But oh, her heart cried, why could he not have loved her in return?

"The cool weather makes them restless," Lorna said.

Miss Anne Preston giggled. "It makes me a bit restless as well," she said, her voice just above a whisper. "Though if my Johnny will hurry home from London, he can put his arms around me and warm me up. Then, I believe the restlessness will go away."

Lorna shook a warning finger at her friend, then she glanced across the rectory's cozy drawing room to make certain the Reverend Joshua Preston still dozed in his favorite chair beside the fireplace. "Behave yourself, Anne. What if the vicar should hear you?"

The young lady, who was newly engaged, giggled again. The thin, plain-faced Anne had loved John Williams for most of her twenty-one years, and while Lorna had been visiting at Clement Park, the young curate had finally asked Anne to marry him. "Father will not hear me," she said. "Besides, it was you who brought up the subject of restlessness."

"I was speaking of bees. And well you know it."

Momentarily repentant, the vicar's daughter asked if Jim Stoddard was afraid his bees were not adjusting to their new home.

"He is. And with good cause. This cool summer has had an effect upon more than just the flowers. Many of nature's creatures are behaving oddly, and bees are no exception. Though, to be honest, sudden changes in the weather always upset the hive."

"Then you were serious about the cool weather making them restless?"

Lorna nodded. "Quite serious. Somehow, the bees know they must keep the hive at a consistent temperature to ensure that the queen will continue to lay eggs. So, they do what they must—no matter the cost."

"No matter the cost? That sounds awfully dramatic."

"It is. If the weather gets too hot, the workers use their wings to circulate the air. Often, they literally wear their wings out, then they die. On the other hand, if it gets too cold, they protect the queen by forming a living blanket around her. The outer bees may freeze to death, but they will never forsake the queen or the hive.''

"Oh, my. That is loyalty indeed.''

"Quite true. Theirs is a society in which every creature knows his part, and they all survive by being cooperative.''

"Cooperative, are they? Hmmm.''

From the blush that stole into Anne's cheeks, turning them a decidedly rosy color, Lorna suspected her friend had something other than bees on her mind.

"Speaking of being cooperative,'' she said, reinforcing Lorna's suspicions, "I hope that is what you mean to be.''

"Anne Preston, what have you done?''

"Why, nothing. At least, nothing so very bad.''

"Anne Elizabeth Preston, I know you. You are up to something. Now out with it.''

The young lady sighed. "Very well. I thought you might stop by today, so I asked Father to invite our new neighbor to join us for tea.''

"New neighbor? What new—'' Lorna groaned. "Tell me you do not mean the baron?''

"Have we any other new neighbor?''

Lorna ignored the sarcasm. "I beg of you, do not turn into one of those women who once she is wed, cannot rest until she has found suitable partners for all her friends.''

"But you are my dearest friend. Why should I not wish to see you happy?''

"But I *am* happy.'' Though the falsehood sat ill upon her tongue, Lorna did not wish to be thrown at some stranger's head.

If Anne doubted the veracity of Lorna's remark, she kept her doubts to herself. Instead, she spoke of the neighbor, whose hiring of the long-vacant Herndon Hall had fueled the village gossips for a full month. "He arrived two days ago," she said, "quite unexpectedly, to see how the renovations are coming along at the Hall."

"And are they? Coming along, I mean?"

"I should think so, considering the number of workmen employed to make the place liveable. But it is not the house I wish to discuss, it is the baron. Lord Nevin, I should say."

"You have met him, then?"

"Not yet. Of course, with Father being the vicar, he thought it only proper that he call upon a new parishioner, so he drove the gig over to the Hall yesterday afternoon to introduce himself to the gentleman."

Despite Lorna's lack of interest in being thrown at Lord Nevin, she was as curious as the next person to know more of this newcomer who had put so many of the village craftsmen to work, promising them bonuses if the work was completed on schedule. "What did the vicar think of the gentleman?"

"Oh, Father liked him. He thought the baron a most personable fellow."

"Personable?" Lorna raised her eyes heavenward, for the saintly vicar used that word to describe nearly everyone he met. "Would you care to wager," she said, "upon the likelihood of the baron's possessing fewer than half his teeth and a decided squint?"

Though Anne giggled, she would not admit it to be at all likely. "I am persuaded that he is a most handsome gentleman."

"Very optimistic of you, my dear Anne, but do consider the facts. He is a gentleman in possession of an old and respected title, and yet he is still unwed. Such a circumstance can only mean that he is unhandsome, unlikable, or both, for you know there are heiresses by the dozens willing to marry a man who can make them a baroness."

"I refuse to share your pessimistic view. Besides, it is said the baron has inherited a fortune with his new title."

Lorna laughed. "Say no more, for we all know the blinding effect a handsome fortune has upon a homely face and a sour disposition."

Anne would not allow it to be so. "I have already decided how it will be. The baron will prove to be as handsome as a Greek god—far handsomer than the miniature of Paul Clement—and the moment Lord Nevin meets you, he will fall madly in love with you and beg you to accept his hand in marriage."

"I hesitate to burst your romantic bubble, but wealthy barons, even the not-so-handsome ones, do not beg the daughters of wool merchants to marry them."

"But—"

"Please, Anne, I implore you, do not introduce me to the gentleman's notice."

"But why?"

"Because," Lorna replied quietly, "I do not wish it."

Lorna hated to disappoint her friend, but she did not want to figure romantically in anyone's daydreams of love and great wealth. She had dreams of her own, though her dreams were of love alone, for she had no need of greater wealth.

With a start, Lorna realized that she had never once wondered about Stephen's financial status. He had never mentioned the subject, and she had never asked. It had not seemed important. Though she had learned at an early age to be suspicious of young men who saw only her dowry, when she was with Stephen, the thought had never crossed her mind. He was her friend, and an honorable man, and she trusted his motives. Even after all that had happened, she still trusted him.

If Stephen had fallen in love with her, it would have been a genuine emotion, not one motivated by money. *If* he had fallen in love with her. Unfortunately, he had not done so, and all her papa's money would not relieve the dull ache inside Lorna's chest.

Her thoughts were interrupted by the sound of hoofbeats outside the rectory. Anne must have heard them, too, for she excused herself, crossed the room to where her father slept, then tapped him gently upon the shoulder. "Father," she said, "wake up. I believe Lord Nevin has arrived."

Reverend Preston blinked several times, then he looked up at his daughter and smiled. "I must have dozed off, my dear. Did you say that our new neighbor had arrived?"

The knocker sounded at the front of the house, answering the vicar's question, and the kindly pastor rose and straightened his neckcloth. Within a matter of seconds the maid scratched at the drawing room door.

"Enter," the vicar called. When the servant opened the door, the Reverend Preston went forward, hand outstretched to greet the tall, broad-shouldered man who had come to tea.

"Lord Nevin," he said, shaking the younger man's hand, "so glad you could come. Please allow me to make you known to my daughter, Anne."

The gentleman bowed toward Anne. "Miss Preston," he said.

Anne curtsied. "How do you do, my lord?"

"And this," the vicar added, "is my daughter's friend, Miss Lorna Maitland."

The newcomer bowed to Lorna. "Miss Maitland."

Lorna could not speak, for her tongue lay like some lifeless object, filling her mouth yet not fulfill-

ing its function. Mutely, she stared into the dark eyes
that smiled down at her—eyes that fit so perfectly in
the ruggedly handsome face, the very same face that
filled her waking thoughts and haunted her dreams.

"How do you do?" Lord Nevin asked.

"Sir," she muttered at last, "I . . . I . . ."

"Yes?" he asked. "You . . . you . . . what?"

When the corners of his mouth began to twitch, as
if he tried in vain to hide his laughter, Lorna knew an
almost overpowering desire to box his ears. "Stephen
Rutledge," she said, anger loosening her tongue,
"this had better not be another of your jests."

Chapter Fifteen

"It is no jest," Stephen replied. "Do you find it amusing, my being here?"

Not in the least! Lorna had no desire to laugh. If anything, she wanted a good cry to purge these confusing emotions that were making a May game of her insides. She neither laughed nor cried, of course, for how could she explain such unseemly behavior to Anne and the vicar. Instead, she asked the man she had thought never to see again, "Why are you here?"

"Why? Because I promised to take young Thomas fishing, and I never to go back on my word."

Miss Anne Preston, obviously perceiving some prior acquaintance between her best friend and the handsome peer, bethought herself of a theological question that had been plaguing her soul—a question that prompted her to ask the vicar if she might have a private moment with him. After casting Lorna a knowing glance, the young lady whisked her father to the far corner of the room.

"What is it, my dear?" the kindly gentleman asked. "What has so perplexed you that you must needs ask it now?"

"It is . . . er . . . er . . . consubstantiation and transubstantiation," the young lady announced rather quickly. "I find I do not understand the difference between the two beliefs."

The vicar stared at his only child. "But, my dear, we have guests. And though I understand one's wish to know more of these quite fascinating religious questions, I really do not think this the proper time to—"

"Please, Father, I know Lorna and Lord Nevin will be so kind as to excuse us for just a few minutes, for I really wish to know the part the wine plays in each concept."

With a sigh, the vicar removed a book of Fordyce's sermons, thumbed through the dog-eared pages until he found what he sought, then handed the volume to his daughter. "Read that," he said, tapping his finger against the right-hand page. "I believe it will clarify the whole."

"Oh, no!" Anne said, catching her father by the sleeve before he could return to his guests. "You read it to me. Please. Theological ideas always sound so much clearer when they come from your lips."

Lorna heard no more of her friend's rather sudden and certainly spurious religious enthusiasm, for she was attempting to make heads or tails of what Stephen was saying. Something about a great-uncle he had not seen in years, and family business matters that had taken him to Derbyshire and detained him there. "And that is how I came to be the new Lord Nevin," he said, as if concluding a quite lucid account of his activities during the past two and a half months.

Lucid or not, his story did not come close to answering the questions that echoed inside Lorna's brain, for those questions had more to do with why a bachelor had hired a large house? And why, of all places, in Plemstock, her village?

"I do not understand," she said, "why, if fishing with Thomas was your object, you must needs hire a house and begin extensive renovations. Do you mean to—"

"Lord Nevin," his host said, raising his voice so he might be heard across the room, "if fishing is your passion, I am persuaded you will find no better sport than here, in the waters of Oxfordshire." The reverend gentleman returned the book of sermons to his daughter, then he hurried back to sit with his guests.

Naturally, their host's presence prohibited any further personal comments between Lorna and Stephen, so the conversation turned to the many sights and entertainments of the neighborhood. For the next hour, while Lorna pretended to drink tea and nibble at a macaroon, she spoke little, choosing instead to listen. By so doing, she gleaned a number of tidbits about Stephen and his plans from his answers to Anne's numerous and increasingly indecorous questions.

Yes, he danced.

Yes, he had every intention of attending the monthly assemblies.

Yes, it looked as if the renovations to Herndon Hall would be finished within the next three weeks.

No, he had no wife.

No, he had no fiancée.

Because Stephen answered all of Anne's impertinent questions without displaying the least sign of having taken offense, there was nothing Lorna could do but sit quietly and allow her friend to interrogate him as though he were a witness before the court.

Finally, Anne asked a question that would have been audacious had it come from an acquaintance of long standing, never mind a young lady the gentleman had only just met. And though neither the questioner nor the questioned seemed at all discomforted, Lorna feared her entire body might burn to cinders with the heat of her embarrassment.

"Tell me, Lord Nevin," Anne said, "since you will wish to secure the succession, may I assume you have not turned your face against marriage and a family?"

"Why, no," Stephen replied. "As a matter of fact, I have hopes of fixing my interests with a young lady in the not too distant future. All that hinders me from putting my luck to the test is an unfortunate misunderstanding that arose—"

Lorna could sit still no longer. Not caring that she interrupted Stephen's reply, or that the vicar and Anne would think her deranged, she stood abruptly and placed her cup and saucer on the tea tray, sloshing half the untouched brew onto the silver cake plate. "Thank you," she said, curtsying to the vicar, "for allowing me to stay to meet our new neighbor. However, I really must be going now. Father is expecting me."

"Oh?" Anne said, the look on her face reminding Lorna of a cat toying with a mouse, "must you go so soon? I had several more questions for our new neighbor. Surely you would find his answers of interest. As for me, I find myself positively agog to know more of him and the mysterious lady to whom he refers."

She turned to Stephen, who had stood politely when Lorna rose. "You have no objection to further inquiry, do you, Lord Nevin?"

"Not at all, Miss Preston. If either you or Miss Maitland wish to ask me something—anything—please do not hesitate to do so. I promise to be as forthright as possible."

Though the remark was addressed to Anne, Stephen looked directly at Lorna. "I . . . I have nothing to ask," she said, "and I really must go. Good-bye, Anne. Vicar. Lord Nevin."

Lorna gathered her leather gloves and her riding

crop, then giving her hostess no further opportunity to detain her or even to escort her to the door, she hurried from the room.

Finding the groom waiting for her in the lane that ran beside the front garden of the rectory, Lorna bid him toss her into the saddle with all speed. The startled servant obeyed, of course, but what he thought of her unseemly bolt from the rectory, or her wish to make a hasty trip back to Epping Grange, Lorna did not bother to ask.

Once her foot was positioned in the stirrup, and she had hooked her left knee over the pommel, then wedged her left foot snugly behind her right calf, she tapped the mare with her riding crop and galloped down the lane, leaving the groom to follow her as quickly as his indifferent mount would allow.

The mad dash from the rectory lasted only a few minutes, with Lorna's riding skill putting her way ahead of her groom, but after the initial run, Lorna regained a semblance of sanity and slowed the speeding mare to a more modest pace. No matter what Stephen Rutledge had said about hoping to fix his interest with a young lady, that was no reason for Lorna to risk injury to herself and the mare.

By the time she reached the brick columns that stood on either side of the entrance to the carriageway of her home, she had convinced herself that she was acting like the veriest widgeon. After all, Stephen Rutledge's unexpected move to Plemstock might have absolutely nothing to do with her. Furthermore, the young lady he mentioned might be anyone. Reason told Lorna that if he had meant to imply that *she* was that lady, he would have found some more private way of declaring himself.

Suddenly spying a gray horse and silver cabriolet that stood alone and unattended near the portico, Lorna reined in the mare, choosing not to ride all the way to the front of the house and risk frightening the unknown animal. Instead, she waited for the groom to catch up with her so he might walk the mare back to the stable.

"Do you recognize that equipage?" she asked the servant. "To whom do the horse and carriage belong?"

"I've never seen it before, Miss Lorna."

The groom slid off his horse, then came around to assist Lorna to dismount. "A right peculiar thing, though, that didn't nobody come from the stables to see to that horse. What Mr. Maitland will say of such behavior, is more than I can—"

"Cousin Lorna!"

Lorna stepped away from the mare in time to see Thomas running toward her at full speed. He came from the general direction of the little informal garden that was a favorite spot with the family members, but if his frightened look was anything to judge by, his sojourn there had not been pleasant.

"Thomas," she said, catching the youngster by the shoulders to steady him, "what is amiss?"

"It's him," Thomas gasped. "It's Treherne." The lad gulped a breath of air. "He is in the garden with Mama, and he is . . . he is threatening her." Tears began to stream down his freckled cheeks. "I came to get Cousin Calvin."

Lorna turned Thomas toward the house and gave him a gentle shove between his thin shoulder blades. "You go find Papa. I will go to your mother."

The boy nodded, then while he hurried toward the front door, Lorna lifted the hem of her riding skirt and ran toward the garden. Once there, she passed beneath the ivy-covered arch that gave access to the rustic area, then she stopped beside a row of box-woods bordered by beds of hearty pink thrift and unpretentious blue delphiniums.

Not ten feet away, near a bent twig settee, stood a rather stocky man of about fifty. He wore a corbeau green coat and buff-colored inexpressibles, and upon his orange-red hair sat a curly brimmed beaver the exact green color of the boxwood. The man's back was to Lorna, and just a few feet in front of him stood Analise.

The stranger's rather coarse voice was raised in anger, and he shouted at the beautiful woman before him. Analise's face was chalk white, and she trembled from head to foot; not, Lorna suspected, because the wind had picked up, making a cool day turn decidedly chilly. Fear made Analise shiver. In all likelihood, she was not even aware of the temperature or of Lorna's presence, for she did not take her eyes off the man in the green beaver.

"I never meant to anger you," she said, her voice weak, but placating. "I should not have allowed you to pay my bills. It was misleading of me, I realize that now, but I was—"

"But me no buts," the man interrupted. "What's done is done, and you'll not play fast and loose with me. No one makes a fool of Felix Treherne. My money was good enough for you then, and now you'll settle the debt by coming with me. What say you to Brighton? A bit of sea air is what we want. Just you and me, my pretty, for a fortnight, or maybe a month. You'll not be sorry, for I'm a man as knows how to treat a woman."

"Is this the way you treat them?" Lorna asked, "by frightening them half out of their wits?"

The man wheeled around. "What the—"

"Analise," Lorna said, her tone as condescending as any Lady Clement had ever used, "do not bother to introduce this person to me, for I cannot think he will remain at Epping Grange long enough for me to have need of his name. As we speak, Thomas is fetching Papa, and the groom should be here any minute with two or three of the brawnier stable lads, on the chance that their services might be needed."

She turned then to Felix Treherne. "I would suggest that you leave the premises before the men get here."

Treherne puffed up like a toad. "Here, now. Who are you to be telling Felix Treherne what he should and shouldn't do?"

Lorna opened her eyes wide, feigning innocence. "Tell you what to do? Nothing of the sort, my good man. Mine was but a suggestion, advice intended to insure that you leave the estate in the same robust good health you enjoyed when you arrived."

The man took a step toward Lorna. "Threaten me, would you?"

"My daughter is too much a lady ter threaten anyone," said an angry voice from just behind her. "But I'm no gentleman, and I'm willing ter offer threats aplenty, along with a few well aimed punches, if that's what it takes ter knock some sense into that thick head of yours."

"Calvin!" Analise cried. She had stood mute while Lorna spoke to Treherne, shivering like a frightened rabbit, but at sight of the girl's father, Analise ran past the man who threatened her, and threw herself upon the chest of Calvin Maitland.

"Oh, Calvin," she sobbed, "I knew you would come to save me. Make Felix go away."

"Calm yourself," he said, patting the weeping damsel on the shoulder with all the finesse of a nine-hundred-pound bear. "I know you're frightened, but there's no need. Just stand aside, there's a good girl, and let me handle this . . . this . . ." Calvin Maitland uttered a crudity worthy of a man who had learned of life the hard way, then he stared directly at Treherne.

"My solicitor has been looking for you for the better part of the summer," Calvin said. "He has a draft for you covering the money you expended on Mrs. Whidby's behalf. If there are further monies owed, you've only ter give the bills ter the solicitor and he will see you are reimbursed. Now get off my land, and never bother this lady again."

Felix Treherne's face grew as red as the hair beneath his green hat, and he muttered an obscenity of his own. "Now see here, you great lummox, you cannot just pay me off like some lackey and expect me to disappear."

"That is exactly what I expect."

While the two men took one another's measure, staring at each other like a couple of angry bears more than willing to do battle, Lorna heard a familiar hum in the not-too-distant background. It sounded for all the world like a bee swarm. Though surely it was a trick of the ear, for bees usually swarmed in the spring or the early summer, not when the weather was this chilly.

That tidbit of information had no more than crossed her mind when Lorna realized that bees had their own ways of doing things, and facts based upon observable apiarian habits were not altogether reliable. Had she not that very afternoon warned Jim Stoddard that unseasonably cool weather made the bees restless? Obviously Lorna needed to consider that warning herself, for at that very instant she spied the queen bee, who had just flown into the garden.

The queen, raised on a diet of royal jelly, was larger than the worker bees, and her size made her unmistakable. Under normal circumstances, she would not leave the hive, but should the colony grow overcrowded, she might seek to start a new colony elsewhere. And where the queen bee went, the workers followed.

While Lorna held her breath, hoping the queen would fly elsewhere, the royal insect hovered just above Felix Treherne's curly brimmed beaver. Obviously attracted to the green color, the queen appeared to be thinking over her options. She hovered, then she flew backward for a moment, then came forward again. Finally, her decision made, she lit right in the middle of Felix Treherne's hat.

"Please," Lorna said, "everyone be very still."

"See here," Felix began, "you can't tell me—"

Calvin Maitland silenced him with a raised hand. "Quiet, you fool." Then to his daughter he said, "What is it? What do you hear?"

"A swarm," she replied. "The queen is here and the workers cannot be far—"

She got no further, for the buzzing grew suddenly louder, and the swarm of bees appeared as if from nowhere—at least two hundred of them. Obviously most of the colony had stayed behind to rebuild with a new queen, for as swarms go, this one was small. Still, two hundred bees flying in unison was a frightening sight, for together they resembled some large, predatory bird.

"Lorna," her father called softly, "come away."

"Fiend seize it!" Treherne yelled when he saw the swarm headed directly for him.

Eyes as wide as an owl's, he had the look of a man about to run. "Be still!" Lorna ordered, the firmness in her voice brooking no disobedience. "Do not move. Not so much as an inch."

She did not have to say more, for the entire swarm began to settle on Felix Treherne's hat, shielding the queen with their bodies to keep her warm. The man beneath all that activity appeared frozen with fear, and he could not have moved if he had wanted to do so.

"Lorna," Calvin tried again. "Please, come away."

"Papa, you know I cannot leave this man."

"You can, my girl. I want you to. I promise you, no one will think any the less of you for not risking your own safety. Come away now, while you still can."

"Oh, me," Treherne muttered, his lips quivering like an old man's, "oh, me."

"Hush," Lorna said. "If you wish to escape unharmed, you must listen to my instructions and do exactly as I say."

"Do it!" Calvin Maitland said, his words an unmistakable order. "My daughter knows about beekeeping, and she is your only hope of escaping the swarm. But I warn you," he added, his voice colder than Lorna would have thought possible in her loving father, "you do anything to turn those bees on my daughter, and I will yank your lungs out with my own hands."

"And when he is finished with you," said a deep voice Lorna recognized immediately, "you have my word on it, Treherne, I will shoot you down like a mad dog."

"Rutledge," Calvin said, "do not go closer."

"I have no intention of doing so," Stephen replied. "I trust Lorna to do what is wisest. I merely wished to add my warning to yours, just in case the gentleman should decide to try his luck at running away."

With the arrival of the swarm, Lorna's heart had begun to race, but it was nothing compared to the acceleration caused by the sound of Stephen's voice. Even if she had wanted to, Lorna could not have stopped herself from turning to look at him. His dark eyes revealed not the least hint of his usual good humor, and she could not be certain, but she thought the coppery hue of his skin appeared just the least bit paler.

"Please," she said quietly, "take Papa and Analise and leave the garden. All of you."

"Not bloody likely," Stephen muttered beneath his breath. Aloud he said, "Not if all the fiends of hell should join us. I shall remain until you are ready to leave. Now get on with whatever you plan to do, for I warn you, I am frightened out of my wits."

"As am I," her father added.

Lorna could not help herself, she chuckled. "Is that castanets I hear? Is there a Spanish dance troop nearby?"

Neither gentleman appeared in the least amused by her little joke. Knowing there was nothing more she could say to persuade those two unquestionably brave men to leave her, Lorna turned back to Treherne. His once green beaver was literally covered by bees, and the man beneath the now yellowish-brown hat had no need to advise anyone of his fear, for he had the look of a man who might faint at any moment. His face was ashen, and his eyes were rolled back in his head.

"Treherne!" Lorna said, the harshly spoken word causing a few dozen bees to fly above the hat before settling once again. "Look at me. Concentrate on my face. If you should faint, and the hat should fall, dislodging the queen, believe me, the workers will sting you until the very last bee is dead."

Treherne's only reply was a moan.

"Do you understand me?" Lorna asked.

"Y . . . yes." He did as she bid him and looked at her. "I understand."

"Good. You must listen carefully to my instructions, and you must do exactly as I say, the instant I say it. No questions. No hesitation."

"I . . . I will do as you tell me. Just get me out of here, and I will give you anything you want."

"We want only one thing from you, Treherne, for you to go away and not bother Analise again."

"I will go," he said. "Just do not leave me to the mercy of these bees. The last time I was stung, the poison rendered me unconscious. This many stings might kill me."

Lorna was very much afraid he was right. "Very well," she said. "I know what I am doing, so do not distract me with questions. When I begin to move toward you, I will speak as little as possible, and I do not want you to say a word. Blink if you understand my instructions."

When the man blinked his eyes, Lorna took the first step toward him. Moving slowly and deliberately, she covered the dozen feet or more that separated them. Under normal circumstances, the distance was negligible, but with two hundred nervous honeybees waiting, the walk seemed to take hours.

Lorna was not afraid of bees, but like all beekeepers, she had a healthy respect for the industrious insects. Even under controlled situations, when she was covered from head to foot by her protective clothing, she still received the occasional sting. Now, with nothing but her long-sleeved habit and her leather riding gloves to protect her, she knew she might be the recipient of a nasty surprise or two.

When she was within arm's reach of Treherne, she paused. "My plan," she said just above a whisper, "is to take the brim of your hat in both my hands."

At the fearful widening of his eyes, Lorna said, "Do not worry, I will not try to remove the beaver, merely hold it steady. When I give you the signal, I want you to sink to the ground. Slowly. Very slowly. Can you do that?"

"Y . . . yes," he whispered.

"Whatever you do, you must not touch me in any

way. If you should bump against me the least little bit, you might make me drop the hat on you."

"No," he said, "I will not touch you."

Without another word, Lorna reached out both arms and slowly slid her fingers beneath the tiny soft bodies of the worker bees until she could grasp the brim of the hat. Once she had as firm a grip as was possible, she said, "Now, Treherne."

Chapter Sixteen

True to his promise, Felix Treherne did not touch Lorna. He must have been a powerful man, for a lesser man's muscles would not have allowed him to move so slowly. When he was on the ground, he whispered, "All clear."

"Good. Now roll away from me, for I mean to stoop down and set the hat on the ground just in front of my feet."

The man lost no time in doing as she bid him. In fact, he did not stop with one roll, but rolled and rolled, not ceasing until he collided with the base of a beech tree some six feet away.

With the hat still held out straight in front of her, Lorna began to bend her knees. She prayed she would have the strength Treherne had exhibited, for she did not want to think about what would happen if she lost her balance and fell upon the hat.

She had only moved the least bit when she felt Stephen's presence. She had always been able to sense when he was near, for he exuded vitality and strength, and Lorna could feel those qualities from several feet away.

Almost as if he knew exactly what she needed, he stepped close behind her, his chest flush with her back, then he reached his arms around either side of her and caught her wrists in his strong hands. His added strength kept her arms from quivering, and as she bent her knees, she felt Stephen's firm body behind her, supporting her as she inched her way to the ground.

At last she was able to bend forward and set the hat on the grass. Even so, she took the same care in releasing the brim as she had in gripping it, and when her fingers were finally an inch away from the beaver and the swarm of bees, she let out her breath in one loud whoosh.

Lorna thanked heaven that Stephen was behind her, helping her to rise, for her knees felt as though they had turned to jelly, and she was not certain she could have straightened without his assistance. When she was on her feet at last, she turned directly into Stephen's waiting arms.

"Is it safe to get up now?" Felix Treherne called from where he lay at the base of the beech tree.

"Get up," Calvin Maitland said. Unfortunately, his voice was so hoarse he was obliged to swallow twice before he could finish what he wanted to say. "Get off my land, Treherne, and never let me see your face again."

The man stood, albeit slowly, then moving cautiously, he walked toward Calvin and Analise, keeping as much distance as possible between himself and the swarm of bees now settled upon his hat. Once he was out of harm's way, he turned and called to Lorna. "Thank you, miss, for saving my life. And don't worry, Felix Treherne is a man of his word. I'm going now, and I'll never bother Analise again."

He raised his hand to tip his hat. When his fingers found only air, he shuddered, as if realizing anew why he was hatless, then he turned and ran from the garden.

"I never want to taste honey again as long as I live," Calvin Maitland declared to the other four occupants of the sunny yellow drawing room.

"Nor I," Analise said.

As for her son, that freckle-faced young gentleman was much inclined to think honey the sweetest, the most wonderful food in the world, and he vowed to eat it every day for the rest of his life. He had not stopped grinning since he had heard Calvin Maitland bark instructions to his mother, informing her in no uncertain terms that she was to consider herself and her son permanent residents of Epping Grange until such time as he could build her a home of her own on the property.

"You've no more notion than a hedgehog how to get on in the world, Analise, and for the boy's sake, I want you here where I can look out for you both. I want no more visits from the likes of Felix Treherne, and I do not want to be worrying all the time that you'll outrun your money and get into another dreadful scrape."

Analise offered no argument to the plan. She asked only that when choosing the site for her house, Calvin pick a spot as far from the apiary as possible.

The heroine of the day had nothing to say upon the subject of honey or houses; all she wanted to do was be alone with the tall, dark-haired gentleman who stood beside the handsome slate fireplace.

Stephen had said very little to her since they left the garden. After Lorna rose from setting the hat on the ground, Stephen had held her close for what seemed an eternity; however, once he had released her and allowed her to go to her father, who engulfed her in a bear hug that threatened to break her ribs, it appeared the new Lord Nevin had run out of things to say.

To Lorna's surprise, it was Thomas who forced Stephen to join the conversation. "Sir?" he said, "you do not seem your usual self. Are you and Cousin Lorna still friends?"

The question must have surprised him, for he looked directly at Lorna, his gaze holding hers, as if he waited to see what she had to say on the matter. From the intensity of the look he gave her, he half feared her answer. "What say you, madam. Have my actions given you a dislike of me?"

"A dislike of you! Of course not."

"You are certain?"

"Quite," she said.

He breathed a sigh of relief. "Good."

A dislike of him! If only he knew. Lorna liked him so much she thought her heart might break if he did not ask to be alone with her—and soon.

Stephen must have been of a like mind, for he crossed the room to stand in front of her, then he held out his hand. "Come, my friend," he said, "walk with me to the stables. When I arrived at your home and heard the commotion in the garden, I abandoned my horse with undue speed. Now I feel the need to see for myself that he found his way to shelter."

Though Lorna could have assured him that one of the stable lads would have taken every care of his mount, and that the gelding was probably munching oats at that every moment, the idea of a look-in at the stables offered as good an excuse as any to quit the room.

"By all means," she said, "let me show you to the stables."

She placed her hand in his and allowed him to assist her to rise, and though the contact lasted only a matter of moments, the warmth of his palm against hers caused tiny trickles of sensation throughout Lorna's body. It was a marvelous feeling, made even more so because she had thought never again to know his touch.

"We shall return shortly," she said, but her father

and Analise did not hear, for they were arguing over the possibility of Analise journeying to London to choose the furniture for her new house.

"I will tell them," Thomas said.

After a wink at the boy, Stephen ushered Lorna from the room and out of the house. Once they were in the open air, they discovered the sun balanced on the edge of the horizon. It had not yet slipped over onto the other side, and as a result, the sky was ablaze with varying hues of gold and orange and red.

As the two concerned horse lovers turned to stroll down the bark-strewn path that led to the stables, Lorna took one last look at the sky, then she sighed. "I love this time of day."

"I love any time of day," he replied, his voice suddenly husky, "if you are in it."

As if he could wait no longer, Stephen gripped her shoulders and spun her around to look at him. "Never do anything like that again! Promise me!"

Lorna did not need to ask him what he meant, for the anguish in his eyes told her plainly that he referred to her handling of the bees in the garden.

"When I saw you reach for that hat, and I imagined your soft skin being stung by hundreds of angry bees, my chest burned as if the stings were even then invading my heart."

With Stephen's hands upon her shoulders, Lorna felt those tiny prickles return, only this time, with him looking into her eyes as if he could not get enough of seeing her, the prickles grew to a veritable flood of emotions.

"Promise!" he said again.

"I will do so, but only if you will promise me something in return."

"Anything," he said.

"No. Do not speak too quickly, for I will ask you one question, and you must answer it honestly, without reservation. No matter what the truth may be, I need to hear it."

He searched her face, as if he might discern ahead of time what she would ask. Finally, he said, "What would you like to know?"

"In your letter, the one you sent to me the evening of that wretched engagement party, you wrote that you wished three things for yourself. The second was that I would forgive you, which I do, and the third was that I would never forget that you are my friend, which I will never do."

Lorna swallowed with some difficulty, for facing the truth—good or bad—was never easy. "What I want you to tell me," she said, "what I need to know, is the first wish, the one you left out of your letter."

"Surely," he said, "you know that already."

Recalling the way Stephen had pulled her into his arms once the bees were no longer a threat, holding her against him as though he meant never to let her go, Lorna hoped she knew. She prayed that she was not mistaken, but she needed to hear the words. "I believe I must hear the wish from your lips."

He did not answer right away; instead, he relaxed his hold upon her shoulders, then slipped his hands up the sides of her neck to her face, gently cradling her cheeks and gazing tenderly into her eyes. "My first wish," he said softly, "is that you might love me as I love you."

Lorna grew weak with relief. "You love me?"

"Oh, yes," he said. "From the first moment I saw you. Even earlier, I think, only I did not know it."

Joy filled her heart, but she had to ask, "When did you begin to suspect?"

He smiled then, and the light in his eyes made the breath catch in Lorna's throat. It was the first time he had smiled since he had arrived at Epping

Grange, and it was the most beautiful sight she had ever seen.

"I began to suspect the true nature of my feelings," he said, "when it occurred to me that I was having fantasies about the various ways I might put an end to Paul Clement's existence."

Finding nothing to dislike in this confession, Lorna chuckled. "You wished to murder him?"

"Oh, yes. Running him through with a sword had a certain appeal, as did throttling him. And that evening when I saw him kiss you, I thought surely I would be obliged to shoot him, for I was damn well not letting him have you. Not without a fight."

"As though I would marry anyone else, when I am so desperately in love with you." Lorna gasped at what she had just said. "I . . . that is . . . do you want to marry me?"

He let his actions speak for him, as he bent his head and softly, slowly brushed his lips across hers, just once. "For my first wish," he said.

The next kiss lasted slightly longer than the first, with his warm lips pressing ever so softly against hers. "For my second wish."

When he bent his head the third time, he let his lips linger, teasing her until she thought she would go mad with longing. "A kiss," he said, "for each of my three wishes. Now, I ask you to make my fourth wish come true, my darling, by telling me that you will marry me."

Lorna's heart began to pound as though it had suddenly found a new reason for its existence. "Yes," she said, "I will marry you."

Apparently pleased with her answer, Stephen claimed her mouth as she had been yearning for him to do, kissing her deeply, passionately, and with such warmth that Lorna thought she might ignite with all the wondrous feeling coursing through her. After a time, when Stephen released her face and wrapped his arms around her, crushing her against him, and molding every last inch of her to his rock-hard body, Lorna decided that if she did ignite, it would be worth it. Anything, just as long as Stephen never let her go.

"My friend," he muttered. "My love. My Lorna."

For a man who wrote such beautiful letters, his vocabulary seemed to have diminished considerably during the past few minutes. Fortunately, the wool merchant's daughter found nothing to dislike in those simple sentences.

"Oh, Stephen," she said, "I love you, too. With all my heart."

Having said everything that was important, Lorna showed Stephen just how much she loved him by wrapping her arms around his waist and turning her face up for another kiss.

PENGUIN PUTNAM INC.
Online

Your Internet gateway to a virtual environment with
hundreds of entertaining and enlightening books
from Penguin Putnam Inc.

*While you're there, get the latest buzz on
the best authors and books around—*

Tom Clancy, Patricia Cornwell, W.E.B. Griffin,
Nora Roberts, William Gibson, Robin Cook,
Brian Jacques, Catherine Coulter, Stephen King,
Jacquelyn Mitchard, and many more!

**Penguin Putnam Online is located at
http://www.penguinputnam.com**

PENGUIN PUTNAM NEWS

Every month you'll get an inside look at our upcom-
ing books and new features on our site. This is an
ongoing effort to provide you with the most
up-to-date information about
our books and authors.

**Subscribe to Penguin Putnam News at
http://www.penguinputnam.com/ClubPPI**